X Q

Wendy can't understand why Ben didn't instantly fall in love with his nephew.

"Ben, instead of being mad at me, why can't you take it as a compliment that I think you'd be a good guardian?" Wendy asked. "That first night, you told me you like a challenge. I can't think of any challenge more incredible than rearing a child. Think of this as an opportunity instead of an obligation."

"All I can think of is I'm going to mess up his little life and twist his psyche. Kids deserve a real family—a mother and a father."

Wendy sucked in a pained breath.

His hand shot out and captured hers. He squeezed her hand gently and softened his voice. "I'm sorry. Some women are happy being on their own, but you strike me as someone who'd rather be with someone. You're too caring to be alone. Since I can't imagine men would ever ignore you, I figure that you're getting over a relationship."

The question in his voice deserved an answer. Wendy looked away. In a muted voice, she said, "My fiancé broke our engagement."

Ben turned her face back to his, stared directly into her eyes, and said succinctly, "The man was a fool."

CATHY MARIE HAKE is a Southern California native who loves her work as a nurse and Lamaze teacher. She and her husband have a daughter, a son, and a dog, so life is never dull or quiet. Cathy considers herself a sentimental packrat, collecting antiques and Hummel figurines. She otherwise keeps busy with reading, writing, baking, and being a prayer warrior. "I am easily distracted during prayer, so I devote certain tasks and chores to specific requests or persons so I can keep faithful in my prayer life."

HEARTSONG PRESENTS

Books by Cathy Marie Hake
HP370—Twin Victories

Unexpected Delivery

Cathy Marie Hake

Heartsong Presents

This book is dedicated to those longing for a child as well as those who already have that taste of heaven in their home. Whether Baby is birthed into a family or brought into it later, that little one is a precious gift from God. I pray you have His patience, wisdom, and grace.

A note from the author:
I love to hear from my readers! You may correspond with me by writing:

> **Cathy Marie Hake**
> **Author Relations**
> **PO Box 719**
> **Uhrichsville, OH 44683**
> **CathyMarieHake@aol.com**

ISBN 1-58660-537-2

UNEXPECTED DELIVERY

All Scripture quotations, unless otherwise indicated, are taken from the HOLY BIBLE, NEW INTERNATIONAL VERSION®. NIV®. Copyright © 1973, 1978, 1984 by International Bible Society. Used by permission of Zondervan Publishing House. All rights reserved.

All of the characters and events in this book are fictitious. Any resemblance to actual persons, living or dead, or to actual events is purely coincidental.

Cover design by Cheri Jetton.

PRINTED IN THE U.S.A.

prologue

"Better you than me, Chuck!" Ben Hawthorne slapped his friend on the back. "Having a baby around would drive me straight up the wall."

"You don't really mean that." Chuck was too proud of his impending fatherhood to listen to anything negative. "Janet and I can hardly wait to have the little one. Last night, she folded all of those tiny clothes and put them in the dresser. She beamed the whole time."

"If it makes her happy, so be it. I'm satisfied with my quiet existence. All I want is a good book, a nice fire, no one to nag me, and no squabbling kids. I'm a confirmed bachelor."

"I said exactly the same thing a year and a half ago."

"The difference is, I mean it." Ben zipped up his parka and gave his friend a self-assured grin. "I've never been the domesticated type. I could cope with being shackled to a woman, but the very thought of kids gives me the willies."

"No one would challenge that," Chuck concurred. Ben Hawthorne was a ruggedly individualistic man who blended in well with their untamed environment. Picturing him with a burp cloth over his shoulder stretched even the most vivid imagination. "Be careful. The weather is shifting."

"The phones aren't working, so just plan on my coming back to take your duty if it looks like the blizzard is turning this direction. That way, you can go on home and snuggle up with Janet to enjoy a little peace before your diapered storm arrives." Ben saluted with a jaunty wave and stepped out into a stiff, Alaskan snowstorm.

Once home, Ben headed for the kitchen. Cooking rated at the bottom of his list of domestic talents, so he opted for eggs again. He cracked the egg into the skillet and grabbed

5

for the pancake flipper, then moaned. He'd done it again—
broken both yokes—so he'd have to hurriedly scramble
them. There must be a trick to this, but he'd never mastered
it. As he swirled the messed-up eggs with the flipper, his
mood darkened. He'd forgotten to spray the pan with non-
stick coating.

He sniffed the acrid smell as two slices of burned toast
popped out of the toaster. Those were the last slices of bread,
so he'd have to eat them or go hungry. Yesterday, he'd reset
the toaster to a higher setting for the last bagel in the house
and forgotten to turn it back. He glanced at the egg carton.
Six left. Just enough to last him 'til his next day off. He
needed to stock up on essentials again. *When I do,* he thought
as he scraped the mangled eggs from the pan onto his plate,
*I'll go to the diner and order eggs. I'll watch how Diane
keeps the yolks whole. Again.*

Since the coffee was decaf, he could indulge in one more
cup before he went to bed. Recalling they were low on coffee
at work, he opened the cupboard, took out an unopened can,
and tossed it over at the door so he'd remember to take it to
the pumping station. A man could do without a lot in life, but
coffee rated as an essential. Scowling at the charred edges of
his toast, Ben decided decent food rated as an essential too.
He'd left a standing order with Howie Kalman to hire a
housekeeper/cook for him. At first, Howie thought he was
joking. He wasn't. He was desperate. All he needed to make
life perfect was hot, home-cooked meals.

He washed his few dishes and left the skillet to soak in the
sink. After taking one last gulp of coffee, Ben bypassed his
computer and headed for his radio. With the telephone on the
fritz, he couldn't call or send E-mails. The radio crackled to
life, and he fiddled with dials.

"Ben Haw—rne?—gle—sons here. Over."

"Yeah, this is Ben. Over." He frowned at the switchboard
and tried to finesse the dials to subdue the static.

"Got paperwork—Sorry—questions—Over."

He shrugged. With the constant barrage of storms they'd been having this year, telephone service had been off more than it was on. He'd cope with this minor inconvenience. On a day when the telephone worked, he'd e-mailed a few questions to Eagleson's regarding another log cabin kit, and they were doing their best to work with him by ham radio. Ben had grown accustomed to patching together fuzzy conversations. He lifted the catalog and stared at the two models he'd narrowed down his choice to: Little Guy or the Baby. They came in pine, spruce, hemlock, and cedar, but cedar had the highest insulation factor as well as high moisture and insect resistance, so that decision was simple.

"I have the basic supplies you listed. Shipping the kit here is no problem. It sounds like the Baby is pretty small. Do you still have the Little Guy? Over."

"Yes. Cute. —ine —ruce— See here—help—ver."

Ben doodled with a dial and winced. The storm front was wreaking havoc with the signal. "Cedar. I've decided to take the Little Guy Cedar model. I have plenty of local help. Over."

A high-pitched whine and more crackles came through, then, "—over."

"I'm losing you. You have all of my particulars on file. Send it ASAP. How long? Over."

"—seven months." The signal died out.

Ben turned off the radio and shrugged. He'd gotten the important information through. With the storm worsening, he'd go back to work and spell Chuck as he'd promised. He had about an hour or so to relax, though. The couch beckoned. He kicked off his boots, propped his feet up on the coffee table, and grabbed a hunting magazine. "Ahhh. Another evening in paradise."

one

The odds are good, but the goods are odd. . . . Wendy remembered her friends' teasing words about finding a husband on this brief trip to Alaska. Now that she was here, she hated to admit to herself those unkind words might hold a kernel of truth. She shivered as she watched the pilot and another man unload the small plane. They must be certifiably crazy for being in shirtsleeves when it was only ten degrees.

Then again, I must be crazy too—thinking of taking a baby on a dogsled ride! Afraid if she lifted her feet, she might slip on the ice, Wendy bounced a bit to warm up and to help soothe Troy. The poor little tyke had been strapped to her chest in a sash carrier for hours. The plane from Fairbanks to Caribou Crossings was only a two-seater, so she'd had to hold little Troy in her lap and stare out the window as the incredibly thick forest gave way to the mind-boggling, vast, white space in this desolate region.

Her arrival at the tiny airstrip had sparked a bit of confusion, but everyone acted quite friendly toward her. Howie Kalman, her pilot, took the lack of planning in stride. Within five minutes, he'd arranged for a dogsled to take her to the Hawthorne cabin. Wendy thought it might be a fun way to travel and soak up some local color until the sled arrived. Suddenly, she reconsidered the wisdom of having a team of sharp-toothed dogs around an infant, but by then, it was too late to chicken out and beg for a good old truck.

"We're almost ready to go," one of the men called to her.

She nodded as she looked at the pile of things they were tucking onto the sled, then smiled down at the baby. "Troy, little buddy, you sure have a lot of junk." Still, Wendy wished they'd had more room on the plane. She'd left Troy's crib, high chair, and two good-sized boxes back in a hangar in Fairbanks. Supposedly, when this little bush plane had a bit of extra space, those essentials would be delivered. In the meantime, Mr. Ben Hawthorne would have to improvise.

After caring for little Troy for more than a month, Wendy had become an expert on improvising. She'd done plenty of baby-sitting as a teen, but that hadn't prepared her for the reality of round-the-clock child care. The first day was fun, the first week turned into a grueling marathon, and she'd finally gotten into a schedule and done pretty well. In fact, she'd lost her heart to the little one.

She lovingly tucked his hood a bit closer around his ears and tried hard to ignore the truth of her situation. She'd stalled for over a week, but the attorney insisted that Hawthorne wanted his nephew. Since she had to relinquish Troy, she needed to come—just to be sure this darling little boy would be in good hands. Maybe then her heart wouldn't ache so badly.

In hopes of sparing Troy's uncle some difficulty, Wendy had the schedule written down and tucked into the side pocket of her purse. She planned to hand it over and give him a few pointers on how Troy liked to sleep, eat, and play.

Her boots slipped through the slush as she made her way toward the back of the sled. The arctic chill radiated up into her feet and legs and bit through the wool sweater she wore. She'd never been so cold. The wonderfully warm coat she'd thought her brother stuffed into the second diaper bag turned out to be another blanket and four extra boxes of diaper wipes. Then again, she planned to leave right away, so that wouldn't be a problem other than for today. At least she'd outfitted little Troy in nice toasty buntings and thermal blankets.

The dogsled man shrugged into a bright red down parka and squinted at the horizon. "We'll have plenty of light to make it."

"Light?"

"We're heading into spring, so the days are getting longer. We have almost another hour and a half of sunlight," he mentioned offhandedly. "Go ahead and climb on board. Here, I'll get the little guy and hand him back after you're situated." He leaned over Troy and frowned. "You'd better bundle him up in another layer of something. This isn't warm enough."

"It isn't?"

"Unh-unh. You need something more too."

"I have blankets in the diaper bag. They'll have to do. You've stuffed everything else onto the sled already." The blankets were barely sufficient for the baby. Pete shook his head, hiked off to a cracker box-sized log cabin, and came back with a hideous, purplish anorak. The fur around the hood looked moth-eaten, but Wendy gladly donned it and breathed a sigh of comfort. "Thank you."

A smile creased his face. "Knew it'd fit. Pretty coat for a pretty girl. Welcome to Caribou Crossing."

Wendy smiled politely at his compliment, though she wondered if she looked half as dreadful as the jacket. Once she tucked Troy in and was situated, they set off. In mere seconds, the sled skimmed over snow and ice like some kind of amusement park ride. Within a short while, the two men Howie had rounded up to help them zoomed up on snowmobiles and waved. Wendy hung onto Troy for dear life, yet she had the urge to do the screw-in-a-lightbulb princess wave. Giggles spilled out of her. Something about the latitude here probably made people loony, and she'd already started to show the symptoms.

Wendy was more than a little surprised when they skidded to a stop in front of a boxy-looking log cabin that literally sat out in the middle of nowhere. She could barely see the roof of another cabin off to the left if she squinted. The snowmobile riders cut their engines and hiked on over. Oblivious to the fact that the utter isolation stunned her, they teased and visited as they started to unpack everything. They all acted exceptionally friendly toward her, and she remained polite; but this was a one-day deal, and Wendy didn't want to encourage any of them to stay behind with her until Troy's uncle got home.

After the temporary elation of speeding across the snow, the awful finality she'd tried so hard to ignore hit her hard—this was where she'd be leaving the baby she cradled to her heart. She needed what little time was left to say her final good-byes to him in private.

To her amazement, no one gave a second thought about walking straight into the unlocked house. In a matter of minutes, they unloaded all the luggage, waved, and disappeared.

Wendy stood at the window and watched until she couldn't distinguish them anymore. At that moment, the reality of her situation nearly overwhelmed her. She was alone. With a baby. In the Alaskan wilderness. Worst of all, tomorrow she'd be gone, and Troy would still be here.

Tears welled up, but she refused to shed them as she snuggled the infant closer. "Lord, help me," she prayed. "Troy belongs to Ben Hawthorne. You lent him to me for only for a few weeks. Help me to give him up."

Wendy cuddled Troy in her arms, cherishing each second. Ben Hawthorne was a very lucky man to be blessed with such a dear nephew. She hoped he'd gotten everything ready, but a quick look around caused her to wonder. Not one single, solitary baby item sat out in the open. It occurred to her that he might have stored them in a closet, but she wasn't about to snoop to find out.

It didn't take long to familiarize herself with the layout of the cabin. The great room measured about twenty feet in each direction. An enormous brown leather couch and two battered navy blue corduroy chairs were grouped around an impressive stone fireplace. Cases filled with books flanked each side of the hearth. An L-shaped kitchen extended around one corner, and an oak trestle table completed the affair. It looked pretty nice, considering it was a bachelor pad.

A compact bathroom and a small laundry room separated two bedrooms. There was also a narrow alcove that contained both a high-tech computer and a jumble of imposing-looking radio equipment and wires. An extra long, queen-sized bed made it clear which bedroom Ben Hawthorne slept in. She opened the door to the other room and winced. All sorts of gear—fishing rods, tackle boxes, guns and ammunition, an ancient set of antlers, and an indoor gym—surrounded the twin bed. A lone sleeping bag sagged over the rod in the wide-open, otherwise empty closet. The only thing that looked vaguely welcoming was the huge bundle of Troy's belongings the men had dumped in there.

"Brrr." She shivered as her breath condensed in the air. The room was freezing. She'd leave the door open so some heat would radiate in. In the meantime, she'd keep Troy bundled up.

Three hours later, she'd relocated Ben's assorted belongings, put Troy's clothing away on the nifty built-in shelves in the closet, and set up the portable playpen. Hungry, she rifled through the refrigerator and found it to be virtually empty. Wendy grumbled as she extracted an anonymous looking hunk of meat and a battered bag of mixed vegetables from the freezer, then gathered odds and ends from the cupboards. While the meat defrosted in the microwave, she prepared a few bottles of formula for the baby so his uncle wouldn't have to do that task this evening. She fed Troy a jar of lamb and rice, then treated him to some pureed plums. By then Wendy was so hungry, she gave serious consideration to eating a jar of them herself.

Troy acted tired, so she sponged him clean, changed his diaper, and put him down in the bedroom. She stood over him and watched as he slept. "Why didn't your mama leave you to me? She never even mentioned your uncle." She blinked back threatening tears and added in an anguished whisper, "Father, I've asked You already. I know I'm supposed to pray for Your will, but all I can do is be honest and speak what's in my heart. You know I love Troy. Please, can't You let him be mine?"

Troy slumbered on his tummy, his little thumb in his mouth and his knees tucked so far underneath him that barely the tip of his toes peeped out beneath his blue-sleeper-clad bottom.

The room had warmed up quite nicely, so she left him in peace.

A stew bubbled on the stove, and Wendy just started to pull biscuits out of the oven when the door blew open and shut again.

"Mmmm. Whatever it is, it smells fantastic!"

A bear of a man completely blocked out the area where the door once was. He had to be one of the largest men she'd ever seen. Wendy nearly dropped the pan she held. She set it down and nervously grabbed a wooden spoon. For a moment, she hoped it was just the bulky parka that made him seem so huge, but once he removed it, a black-and-red plaid wool shirt stretched across shoulders that looked bigger than life.

He walked as if he owned the whole earth. There was an assurance to his bearing, an almost imperial confidence. Although the parka hood had rumpled his slightly wavy, blond hair, it looked appealing instead of mussed up. His blue eyes twinkled. Absurdly enough, he held a can of coffee.

"When I left for work, I never imagined I'd come home to this. What a wonderful surprise."

She let out a silent sigh of relief. This was going far better than she'd dared hope. Maybe the private investigator her brother hired gave them accurate information—Ben Hawthorne really was a nice guy. Though he hadn't expected them to arrive today—and the fact that he'd not been at the landing strip to greet them would support his claim—delight showed clearly on his face. Ben set the coffee down on the counter. Wendy grinned at it and teased, "Good to the last drop?"

A low, rich chuckle rumbled out of him. "Your food or the coffee?"

Her tongue cleaved to the roof of her mouth as he closed the last few feet between them. She didn't answer; she couldn't because Ben Hawthorne slid next to her and leaned one hand on the range as the other hand casually cupped her waist. His deep voice sounded warm and welcoming. "I'm not kidding. I'm delighted you came."

"Yeah?" She turned with a smile and suddenly felt just how close he'd gotten. Her eyes widened as he leaned closer and gently brushed a fleeting kiss on her cheek. He seemed to make time stop momentarily as he greeted her with a very tender salute, not deepening it or grabbing at her, but simply giving her a welcome that could be interpreted as friendly—she hoped. She wasn't going to be here long enough to strike up a relationship, and from what she'd seen so far, her friends were right: Men up here truly were. . .different.

Wendy's mind whirled crazily. She turned her head away and cleared her throat as she fought the tingling heat of a blush. How did someone who had just been outside in the snow manage to have such warm lips?

"Ahhh." Ben purred contentedly. He sensed her surprised reaction to him. She dipped her chin, and several light brown curls fell forward to hide her blush; so he figured she was shy too. Her reaction to that little peck charmed him. He refused to even blink for fear the woman might disappear. If this were a dream, he prayed the alarm clock wouldn't go off.

He'd left that standing order for a housekeeper with Howie, and from the smell of the cabin, his wishes had been granted in the form of this shoulder-high pixie. Her enchanting green eyes sweetened the deal considerably. It had been a lousy day at work. Coming home to her and the fragrant aroma of real food felt like balm on his tattered nerves.

"Howie told me he'd bring you in, but I never thought he'd really manage to get you to come."

"Of course I came." She added a dash of a greenish herb to the stew.

"Hey, I'm glad."

Her waist beneath his hand was trim, and she smelled even better than the food she stirred so nervously. He wanted to let out a low, satisfied whistle. Instead, Ben granted her a broad smile and offered a belated greeting, "Welcome to Caribou Crossing."

"You didn't write back."

Poor gal. The words popped out of her mouth more like a comment than an accusation, but she bit her lip as if to keep from saying anything more. From the way her eyes widened and her cheeks turned a pretty shade of pink, Ben assumed her wits were scattered and a bit of reassurance might be in order. He'd startled her with that friendly little peck, so he took the wisest course of action and let go of her.

"I trusted Howie. He's salt of the earth. Give him a challenge, and he'll invariably rise to it."

She nodded. "He rounded up a dogsled and a few men to get everything here from the airstrip."

"At the risk of repeating myself, that smells heavenly. What is it?"

"It's some kind of meat, but I'm not really sure about the specifics. The package wasn't labeled, but I pulled it out of your freezer and tried to turn it into stew. Your food supply is a little meager."

"Let's see." He snatched the spoon from her and closed his eyes as he savored a small sample. "Perfect! I have plenty of food up in the attic."

She neatly sidestepped and turned around, effectively getting him to give her a bit more space, then scanned the room in surprise. "There's an attic?"

"Uh-huh. I'll show you around later. You have me at a disadvantage. I'm Ben, but you already know that. What's your name, Cookie?"

"Wendy Marbury."

"Wendy, I'm practically drooling over those biscuits. Let's eat."

They sat down to the meal. He noted Wendy silently bowed her head to pray, so he stayed quiet out of respect. His family never sat together at mealtime, let alone prayed, but something about it seemed. . .right. Warm and homey. Though he prayed during his devotions, he never stopped at mealtime to give thanks. Since she'd be eating with him from now on, he'd suggest they take turns and pray aloud at the next meal. *Wow, Lord. You really outdid Yourself. This woman was worth waiting for.*

Most single Christian women wouldn't stay in a cabin with a man. Then again, he'd promised Howie if the housekeeper arrangement worked out well, he'd build her a little cabin of her own. In fact, he'd just ordered the Little Guy in cedar from Eagleson's. She'd undoubtedly consented to staying in the spare room because it was just a temporary setup.

His new housekeeper from heaven took a sip of water, then ventured, "Is there anything you want to know?"

"Not particularly. I figure we'll get to know each other pretty fast."

"I didn't see any of the supplies I wrote about."

"You sent a list?" His brows hiked upward.

"Of course I did. Pardon me for saying this, but you seem so incredibly offhanded and blasé about all of this. Are you usually so easygoing?"

"What's to get excited about? We'll work things out satisfactorily. I just have a gut-level feeling about it."

Wendy shook her head in wonder.

He tipped his spoon at her and decided, "You're obviously not from around here."

"Of course not." His comment baffled her.

"No one around here has your coloring. I'm the only blond. There's Chuck's wife, Janet—she's got reddish hair. Everybody else is Athabaskan."

"Athabaskan?"

"Native."

"Oh. Eskimo."

He shook his head. "Eskimo, Aleut, Athabaskan, Tsimshian, and a few other native tribes live up here, but each is proud of its distinct heritage. This was originally an Athabaskan settlement, and the pipeline employees have joined the community."

She bobbed her head understandingly. "Okay. I got you." She looked around and smiled at him. "Your house is nice and cozy."

"Thanks. I made it from a kit."

"That's a joke, right?"

He shook his head. "Several companies specialize in making log cabins. They have ready-made kits or oncs you can customize. This came with everything labeled and numbered. It took four of us nine days to get it completely done, including thc plumbing. The electrical took me a little longer, but I thought it was kind of fun. I like a challenge."

"I guess that explains a lot," she said, thinking of his breezy acceptance of Troy. She buttered a biscuit and popped it into her mouth.

"What about you, Wendy? Do you like challenges?"

"Not really," she confessed, then gave him a tipsy grin. "I'm here, though, aren't I?"

"That you are." He gave her a beaming smile. "And you won't hear me complain one bit. I don't remember the last time I ate anything half this tasty."

"Thank you."

"You have a real talent."

This man is genuinely nice, Wendy thought. *Kind. Gentle. I was wrong to doubt Laura's judgment in assigning him to be Troy's guardian. Lord, if any bachelor could handle the baby, this is the one.* Her qualms evaporated, but the sadness still remained. She ought to say something. "You know, I have to admit I harbored serious misgivings about this whole deal. You have no idea how hard it was to come up here, but I really do think it's going to work out. I can't tell you how important it. . ." Emotions closed off her throat.

"It must have been a difficult step for you," he said in an understanding tone. "It's a big move, and you don't know me from Adam."

She nodded and tried to nibble a bit of the biscuit but found it hard to swallow. They lapsed into a comfortable silence. A few minutes later, Troy started to cry.

"What in the world is that racket?"

"The baby." She grinned and shrugged. "He almost let me

finish eating my meal this time. You may as well come meet him."

"Baby!" Ben boomed in pure outrage. "Howie wouldn't have hired you if he knew you had a baby."

"Hired me?"

Ben set his spoon down precisely and gave her a no-nonsense look. "Listen, you cook great, but I'm not fond of kids. This isn't going to work out."

"You sure have your wires crossed. Howie didn't hire me; I hired him."

"You hired Howie? For what?"

"To bring you Troy."

"Who's Troy?"

"Troy is your nephew."

"I can't have a nephew. I don't have a brother or sister." He gave her a smug smile. "You have the wrong man."

For a moment, his assertion took her aback. Then she remembered what the lawyer told her. "Laura was your stepsister. You did have a stepsister, didn't you?"

His smile melted into a look of total horror. "My nephew? A baby? Oh, no, Lady. Don't you dare try to saddle me with a baby!"

"There's no need to yell at me." Everything inside her revolted. This man didn't like babies? How could she ever let him keep Troy? A small voice in her heart whispered, *You kept him only until he could be here, where he belongs. You've no right to interfere.* She turned her back on him and went to get the child.

Ben's eyes nearly bugged out of his head when she returned with a small, squirming bundle. He went ashen and dropped onto the sofa like a felled tree, covered his eyes, and moaned, "Oh, no!"

"Oh, yes." She steeled herself with a deep breath, then shoved Troy into his uncle's arms.

"Oh, no. Take him back. I'll break him or something."

She'd gladly take him away, but she forced herself to let go.

She needed to fill him in on all of the details and get out of here quickly before she went against Laura's will and ignored God's plan. How could Ben Hawthorne fail to see what a darling baby Troy was? What kind of man didn't love children? His attitude set fire to her temper. "Stop acting like that and feed him. There's a bottle for him there on the coffee table."

"I barely know what end to stuff it in. I'll drown him."

"He's old enough to hold his own bottle. The minute you get it near his mouth, he'll take over, so spare me the theatrics. I'm already frazzled after a long flight."

Glowering at Troy, then giving Wendy the same treatment, he announced, "You can't do this to me. Why should I take him?"

Great question. You don't deserve him. Giving herself a mental shake, Wendy replied evenly, "Because Laura wanted you to rear him."

"Laura is a dingbat if she thinks I'm relieving her of this responsibility."

Wendy froze. Something was very wrong here. After a prolonged silence, she tentatively said, "You spoke with the attorney."

"Huh? I haven't talked with a lawyer."

"Didn't you get the letter from Nagel and Sons?"

"Lady, I'm in no mood for these cute little games. I haven't gotten any letters unless they're in that mailbag on the table. If you have something to say, come right out and say it."

Sympathy softened her heart. She hadn't planned on having to break bad news like this, and she wanted to be sensitive. After whispering a quick prayer for the right words, she said quietly, "Laura and Mike Lansing were killed in an auto accident four-and-a-half weeks ago. Their will stipulated you were to be Troy's guardian."

"What?"

She couldn't tell whether he was reacting to the information about the deaths or to his new responsibility. Wendy stayed silent and let her words sink in.

Holding up his hand, then quickly grabbing for Troy when he started to wiggle away, Ben groaned. He rubbed his temple as if he had a royal headache and focused back on her. "Did I hear you correctly? My stepsister, whom I haven't seen since she was in junior high, just up and died and left me with a kid I didn't even know existed?"

"I suppose that's one way of looking at it."

The baby started wailing at top volume. Obviously overwhelmed, Ben demanded, "Do something."

"Feed him," she urged quietly. "I'm so sorry for your loss. I know it will take time to sink in, but Troy and you can console each another."

"Lady, a screaming kid isn't a consolation—it's a disaster." He shook his head. "Forget this. Take him, calm him down, and let me think."

Wendy gawked at him. Then her heart melted. "I understand. You're in shock—"

"Listen. I'm not going to sugarcoat this." He looked down at the screeching baby, then back at her. "My dad had live-in girlfriends by the score. Laura was different because he happened to marry her mom, so she stuck around a whole lot longer than any of the others. I was finishing high school. Laura and I hardly spent any time together since she went to junior high and because I knew Dad would get rid of her and her mom soon enough. I felt bad for her—she took the breakup hard—so when she sent Christmas cards every year, I figured I'd send her one in return. That is as far and deep as our relationship went. There's no reason on earth for Laura to have thought I'd want her kid."

Aghast, Wendy stammered, "But—"

"Enough talk. Hush this kid up, will you?"

Completely disgusted, she rose, snagged the bottle off the coffee table, smacked it into his hand, and walked out of the room.

"Hey! What are you up to?"

"I'm doing something. I'm letting you feed Troy. He's your charge." She slipped into the spare room, pressed her back to the door, and closed her eyes to dam back the tears. She ached to grab Troy away from Ben and soothe him, but if she started that now, he'd never step in and take care of Troy or get to know him. Walking away and leaving them alone nearly broke her heart.

Lord, I don't understand. He's worse than I imagined. You're asking me to give away that sweet, little boy to a beast. He's so selfish—big and mean too.

≈

Ben stabbed the bottle into Troy's face and grumbled under his breath. Troy acted frantic to eat, but instead of eating, he squalled like a banshee.

Ben felt guilty for not being gentler with the noisy kid. Poor thing was an orphan. Ben awkwardly tried to pat him. Troy's face turned red as a fire engine, and his volume matched a siren. Ben shifted his hold and gruffly said, "Hey, Bud, chill out. C'mon and gimme a break. Chow down, and you'll feel better. Then at least one of us will be all right."

Troy continued to holler.

That woman had to have some trick to calm down the kid. Unwilling to listen to the baby's ear-piercing wails any longer, Ben got off the couch, held Troy as if he were a porcupine, and marched to the door. *Lord, give me patience until I get rid of them.*

He knocked the door open wide with his hip. "You could have at least stayed and helped me. Troy won't eat. I'll bet—" His voice skidded to a halt.

Wendy's eyes were positively huge and shimmered with unshed tears. She obviously never expected he would burst in on her in the bedroom. Color splotched her high cheekbones and nearly made her fair skin glow as she hastily secreted something behind her back. "Get out of here!"

"No. It's my house." His voice came out less than steady as he made that assertion. The fact that he sounded like a thwarted six year old registered, but he couldn't back down. He needed help too much to let go of her—she was his lifeline to sanity.

She backed up a step and dropped a pale blue something into a tiny case.

He took a step forward. "Was that a blanket? Do you think he's cold?"

Her face flamed as she twisted to slam the lid down. "No, he's warm enough."

"Too late, Wendy." He stalked closer. "Hiding long johns from me is pretty juvenile. If you're cold, put them on."

"I planned to, until you thundered in."

"How was I supposed to know you planned to change?" he asked in an exasperated tone.

"You could have knocked."

He sighed. "I apologize for my lack of manners, but I'm desperate. Give a guy a break here, Cookie. You showed up with a baby and dumped him in my lap. I need help, and I'm not going to tiptoe around asking for it."

"I don't mean to sound cruel, but that's your concern now. You'll have to get used to him and his needs. Child care is something you learn simply by doing whatever needs to be done. I'd never baby-sat an infant until I took on Troy's care. Neither had my brother, and he got proficient in just a few days."

"I'm not keeping him for even a few days."

"Dive in—really, you'll do okay."

"Not a chance. I told you, he's not staying, and in the meantime, you have to help me."

She stayed ominously still and silent, then whispered thickly, "Surely you have neighbors somewhere to help you out, don't you?"

"Hey, I'm telling you, I'm not keeping him." He stared at her and winced at the tears filling her eyes again. Dealing with a crying baby was bad enough—but a weeping woman? No, thanks. At least she'd managed to keep from shedding those tears. His best bet would be to ignore them and hope she got her emotions under control. The kid let out a howl. Ben scowled at him, then at the woman. "You'll have to find a new home for this little diapered storm."

"I didn't bring him here so you could window shop and decide if you wanted him after you took him for a test drive. He's not a car; he's a person."

"There's a shame."

"The shame is your attitude. He's an orphan. Your sister trusted you to rear him."

"My stepsister hero-worshiped me from the ages of nine to twelve. After all, I was her older, high school brother, and she thought I was cool and independent. I went away to college, and our parents divorced. I haven't seen her in. . ." He did some quick calculating and grimaced. "Twelve years. Twelve years, Wendy. We lost track of each other right after she got married. The fact of the matter is, I haven't thought of her in ages."

"The more salient point is, Laura thought of you. Of everyone she knew, she trusted you to love her son. She specifically left him in your care."

"I just thought she was noodle-brained because she was young. This proves she didn't have a brain at all. I'm not father material."

"You have to be now."

Heaving a sigh, he lifted the baby a bit higher. The kid didn't weigh more than a ten-pound barbell, but he was the biggest burden Ben had ever held. "Yelling at each other isn't doing us any good. This kid is sobbing his guts out, and I don't have a clue what to do for him."

"Feed him. I gave you the bottle."

"Come to the living room and do it yourself," he commanded gruffly.

"Not on your life."

His patience was spent. "You're acting like a first-class shrew. I probably ought to be glad you're not the housekeeper

I asked Howie to find."

Wendy blanched and stated in a tight, icy tone, "I came here as a favor to my brother."

Her brother? What did he have to do with this? Ben didn't dare ask. Too many relatives were already mixed up in this mess.

"I know my brother wrote you."

Okay, so I can't ignore her brother. He scowled. "What does your brother have to do with anything?"

"He's the executor of the estate. He and I were named interim guardians so Troy wouldn't end up in a foster home. You didn't respond to Bruce's letter, so Mr. Nagel radioed you three nights ago."

"Lady, I haven't talked to Mr. Nagel."

Her eyes glittered—whether from temper or tears, he wasn't quite sure. "He told me all about the radio call. You said you had the basic supplies and to send the kid. You told him, 'See here, I've decided to take the little guy,' and that you have plenty of local help."

Ben smacked his forehead with his palm in horrified disbelief. "I was ordering a log cabin kit—not this kid."

Wendy gaped at him. "That can't be. He said, 'Fine, I'll have Bruce send her,' and you agreed."

Ben grimaced and thought back to the radio call. "This is wrong, all wrong. Eagleson's asked if I wanted pine, spruce, or cedar."

She gave the noisy baby a desperate look. "Obviously you got your wires crossed, because you asked for Troy. They sent me with him because we've had him for a month—"

"A month?" he interrupted. "Then you're good with him."

"The fact that I've learned how to care for Troy isn't the issue. It took us almost a month to find your identity since you don't go by your legal name."

"Hey, I had good reason," he growled.

Before he could cut her off at the pass by changing the subject, she took in a deep breath, squared her narrow shoulders, and continued on. "Stability is vitally important for an infant. He needs to settle in with you. I was merely acting as my brother's agent, delivering Troy to his guardian. Troy's your ward."

"Bluntly put, I don't want him."

"This isn't just an offer for a date that you can turn down. Troy's been legally entrusted to your care, and you agreed to take him when you and Mr. Nagel spoke."

"Miscommunication—it was a colossal misunderstanding. No court in the land would accept a crackling ham radio consent as grounds for adoption. I refuse to sign whatever papers that Nagel guy sent along with you."

"Troy is yours until you iron out those problems, so you need to care for him." Her voice softened, then cracked as she looked at the crying bundle in his arms. "Please feed him. He's really hungry."

"What are you doing?" He watched her shift back a step and wrap her arms around her ribs. "Okay, so you're cold. I'll give you a minute to put on something warmer. Once you're done, you can handle him."

She looked at the baby, and several emotions flickered across her features. "Just go sit on the couch, snuggle him tight, and he'll hold his own bottle."

"Easy for you to say," Ben grumbled.

As he turned around to leave, she said, "Please shut the door."

"Listen, Lady: I have a baby and a bottle. I only have two hands." He left the door wide open as he stalked out.

"Lord God," he heard her pray in a tone that bore more than a tinge of frustration, "he has enough hands; he just doesn't have enough heart."

"I heard that!"

two

"Wendy, get out here! He barfed on me!"

As she emerged from the bedroom to survey the damage, Wendy fought the tightness in her throat and telltale tingling behind her eyes and nose. She had to blink to clear her vision, then blink again to make sure what she was seeing was real.

Ben held Troy like a football in one arm, and with the fingers of the other hand, he pinched the fabric of his shirt and held it away from his skin. His face twisted in disgust.

At the point where she'd either laugh or cry hysterically, Wendy burst into peals of laughter.

"Stop laughing at me. This is all your fault."

She laughed even harder. It wasn't funny at all, yet it was.

Struggling to his feet since he still had hold of his shirt and the baby, he tried to hand off Troy, but she stepped back. "You have to learn to deal with this by yourself. I'll talk you through to make sure you have the basics down."

He started to put the baby down on the couch, but she warned, "Don't leave him there. He'll fall off."

"What do I do?"

"Try putting him in the playpen. You ought to burp him first, though. He has something called reflux, so he gets heartburn and upchucks a lot. Burp him in self-defense. Otherwise he'll spit up on you all over again."

"Spit up? He erupted like Mount St. Helens."

"He's got a hefty appetite but a touchy stomach. Did you let him drink all eight ounces without a break?"

"You said he was hungry. He attacked that bottle with gusto—"

She lifted her hands in a gesture of futility. "Why should this make any sense to you? You probably chug-a-lug twelve ounces of beer in a minute flat."

"I hate beer. It stinks. In fact, I don't drink at all."

"There's a miracle." She felt embarrassed at having blurted that out and added, "You'll be a good example when he gets a little older."

"Lady, if you're looking for miracles, you'd better search at another address. I can tell you here and now, God knows me, and He's wise enough to never dump a baby on my doorstep. Someone got wires crossed, because this little guy and I aren't going to be an item."

Wendy gulped and tried to get Ben to see to Troy's needs. "You'd better burp him. That's the best advice you're going to get from me at the moment. Watch." She slid a diaper onto her shoulder, hiked a teddy bear up there, and patted its back a few times. "See?"

Ben awkwardly followed suit. Letting go of his shirt made the wet patch stick to his chest, and he shuddered dramatically. He whacked Troy once and Wendy let out a yelp. "What's wrong now?" he demanded in a beleaguered tone.

"Hit the poor kid like that and he'll be squished flat. Pat him gently. He's tiny for his age—only weighs thirteen pounds." She watched him try to tame his patting technique and ascertained that it was still too rough. "Better yet, just swirl your hand between his shoulders. No, lower. That's too low. His diaper doesn't need a massage."

"I ought to charge you admission for all the amusement you're getting out of this."

Troy belted out enough noise to rattle the cabin, and Ben manufactured the first smile he'd had since he discovered a baby under his roof. "What a stud!"

"I should have known that would rate some approval." She smiled weakly. "Go lay him down and change him. While he's in the playpen, rinse out your shirt. Formula leaves yellow stains if you don't immediately rinse it out."

"You change him." He looked down at his shirt in utter revulsion. "I'll change me."

"Nothing doing, Hawthorne." She'd been through this with her brother and remembered the episode well. The only way to learn some things was by doing them.

"I'm changing first."

"That's a tactical error."

"So what? I have a feeling I'll make more over the next few days."

She gave him a relieved grin. "So you're finally owning up to your responsibility?"

"Not on your life." He put Troy in the playpen, stripped out of his shirt and undershirt, and clutched them in a white-knuckled fist. After he stuffed them into the washing machine, he paced back and forth across the living room bare-chested.

He has a home gym, she reminded herself. Still, it was hard to keep from gawking at him. He had a physique impressive enough to do one of those vitamin or protein supplement ads. Strength like his could mean safety, or it could spell disaster.

Wendy tore her gaze away. Before she'd let Troy go, she'd demanded Bruce check out this uncle. The report painted him as a paragon of virtue. The investigator promised Ben Hawthorne was harmless. Gentle. Easygoing. He seemed anything but those things. The looks he shot at her and Troy rated as incendiary.

"Baby. Crazy. No way," he muttered under his breath as he paced to his bedroom.

Wendy took several deep, calming breaths. Unfortunately, although they were deep, the calming part was way overrated. She needed to do something. Anything.

Ben disappeared into his bedroom for a jiffy, then reappeared wearing a sweatshirt. As he yanked it down to his hips, he growled, "I just finished working a few extra days and got behind on my laundry. Since I live alone, I'm used to tossing stuff directly into the washing machine." He came a bit closer. "I'm unhappy about this situation, so I got caught up thinking about it. I didn't mean to embarrass you."

She flickered him a halfhearted smile. *I have to leave Troy with him. If we get along, maybe he'll at least keep in contact.*

Each time she thought about giving up the baby, she wanted to weep. Not that it would make any difference. *He couldn't handle a baby crying—he'd probably really lose it if I gave into tears. He'll probably do okay. His house is clean, and he tried to do his best. I made blunders those first hours. My brother was nearly hopeless at the beginning too. This is a sink-or-swim kind of situation. Best I let him handle things on his own.*

Feigning a nonchalance she was far from feeling, Wendy sauntered past the playpen, over to the table. Her stew had gone cold, so she microwaved it, finished it, then washed and dried her bowl. Wendy tucked the remainder of the stew into his empty refrigerator. Fishing through the diaper bag, she commented, "I've written down a schedule so you can keep Troy on an even keel. Once you're done, I'll go over it with you."

"What's that thing you're wearing?"

"A sling."

His forehead wrinkled. "A sling is what David killed Goliath with. What's that?"

"A baby-carrying sling. It's like a big sash with a huge pocket for the baby to ride in. Since he's not tiny anymore, I wear it off to the side so he can straddle my hip. It leaves a hand free so I can get things done. I'm demonstrating it so you'll be able to tuck Troy in and still do whatever you need to get done."

Watching her cruise around with the teddy bear safely tucked against her convinced him that this was a practical product. With Troy in his arms, he felt completely helpless; he feared he was going to drop the kid. Who would have ever dreamed the answer to that difficulty would be so simple? "So why aren't you holding him in it?"

"You'll figure that out in a minute."

"I'll take that up with you later. Where are the diapers?"

"I brought you four packages." She bit her lip for a second, then confessed, "Make that three and a half. Troy went through more than usual today. They're enough to last you for about two weeks. After that, you'd better lay in a supply. Wipes too. They're all in the baby's room."

He declared rashly, "This diaper better be wet. I'm not handling any surprises, if you get my meaning."

"You're going to have to." She watched Ben lift Troy out of the playpen, tagged along behind him, and leaned into the doorjamb for the show. He might not have noticed it yet, but she'd gotten a whiff of exactly what the big man feared the most.

"Okay, Buster. I've had a nightmare of a day. No nonsense, do you hear me?" He laid his nephew down on the bed and gave him a you'd-better-cooperate-if-you-know-what's-good-for-you look.

Troy gave him a goofy smile and babbled.

"A word of advice: Put that waterproof pad under him, or you'll have a bigger mess to clean up."

"Thanks." Ben gratefully did as she bade, then looked at the sleeper with a mixture of dread and determination. Unsnapping it, he said, "I'm ten times your size, and my jeans have fewer buttons than this."

Wendy barely stifled her giggle.

He opened the diaper and growled, "At least give me a nose plug and gloves."

"Sorry, I don't have either. By the way, being a boy, he has a bad habit of—whoops! I guess you just discovered it." Turning, she half raced to the relative safety of the couch while Ben bellowed like a wounded elk.

Wendy heard him mutter, "Listen, Kid, I'm finishing the job only because I can't let that woman witness such an embarrassing defeat."

She applauded softly as Ben reappeared. "I see you managed."

He plopped Troy on the couch next to her and gave her an unrelenting glare as she visually measured the wet patch on his sweatshirt. "I'm changing. Again. Watch that little commando to be sure he doesn't make another mess."

Wendy scooped Troy into her arms and softly cooed to him. She pretended she didn't hear Ben's irritated growl. Pasting on her most innocent expression, she tilted her head to the side. "How could you say anything so mean about such a sweet, innocent—"

"Innocent? Look what he did to me! The way he shoots out of the top and bottom, he should have come with a warning label."

"A warning label?"

"Yeah." He scowled at her and the infant. "Warning: Contents under pressure." When she didn't immediately gush something supportive or apologetic, he gave her a disgruntled look. "You need to get your head examined if you think he's a cherub and I'm a guardian."

"You'll learn how to cope—"

"Oh, no, I won't. If anything, the last ten minutes only underscored everything I've said all evening. I'm not the fatherly kind, and I'm not waterproof. Heaven only knows, if that little rascal had any more openings on his tiny body, they'd leak all over me too."

"You'll get used to minor inconveniences like that."

Ben gave her a dark look that made it perfectly clear he thought she was either cruel or criminally insane.

"Go on and take your shower." She watched him stomp off, then gave Troy a soothing pat. Curling more tightly around the little guy, she comforted, "Give him time. He'll come around."

He cooed at her and tangled his fingers in the ends of her hair.

"Listen up, little guy, no more stunts until I've gotten out of here. Don't get me wrong—I love you—but your mommy wanted you to stay here. I know he'll find any excuse to send you back home with me." She paused and blinked back a rush of tears. Nothing would make her happier, but it was wrong. She swallowed hard and forced her voice into the perky tone Troy loved. "But he's your uncle, and you belong with him. It looks like you'll have to train him just as much as he's going to have to train you."

Troy started gnawing on his knuckles.

"Yep, Sweetie, he'll be chewing his nails within five minutes of me leaving here, but don't let that bother you because even though he acts grumpy, he's doing pretty good."

In truth, Ben Hawthorne had done a fair job feeding and changing Troy. He'd blustered and thundered, but he'd been very careful and gentle when actually handling the baby. Once the shock wore off, he'd manage.

He'd make it through, but Wendy knew in her heart of hearts she'd manage better. Life wasn't fair. Not at all. She'd learned to accept reality and move on, though. The last year taught her how. She'd apply those lessons and resolve to cope—even if she didn't want to. . .even if it would tear her heart out.

Ben didn't just change. He took a shower, and he took his time in it too. He padded back out in a set of gray, fleecy sweats, toweled his hair, and gave Wendy a jaundiced look. "I'm still hungry."

"Go ahead and heat up the stew again. We can go over the schedule, and I can give you some pointers; but you'll have to get busy to line up a baby-sitter for Troy when you work, and I need to get moving."

He stopped towel drying his hair. "Just why should I get a baby-sitter, and what makes you think you're going anywhere?"

She didn't answer the first part of the question. It would only lead to an argument. "The dogsled brought me straight here from the landing strip. I didn't check in at the hotel yet."

"Caribou Crossing," he said as he hung the towel around his neck, "doesn't have a hotel."

"I'm too tired to play games, Ben. Grab your car keys and take me to the hotel."

"We don't have a hotel."

"Every one-horse town has an inn of some kind."

"Caribou Crossing has no horses at all. Dogsleds, snowmo-biles, ATVs—yes. No horses, no hotels, inns, guest houses, hostels, or whatever you want to call them." He crossed his arms and looked at her with a smug expression.

"You're serious!"

"Yep."

Wendy had noticed when they flew in that the town looked dinky, but she hadn't really assessed it. How could Troy grow up in a place so remote they didn't even plan on visitors? She stammered, "What do you have here? A church? A store? What about a school?"

"There's no church. We worship in a community hall that isn't heated most of the time." He shrugged. "The kids up here are homeschooled with computer links and correspon-dence programs. The Rivians run a store out of their house. They're an older couple, and they won't appreciate you both-ering them at nine o'clock at night, wanting shelter. You'll have to stay here."

Seeing no alternative, she rubbed her nose to Troy's and breathed in the sunshine scent of the softener she'd used on his sleeper. "I guess I get to spend one last night with you."

Ben jarred her attention back to himself by asking, "What were you planning to do tomorrow?"

"Leave." *At least, my body will be on the plane, but I'm leaving my heart behind.*

"Oh? And where, pray tell, will you go?"

"Home."

Ben stuck his head in the refrigerator and emerged with the stew pot. As he set it on the range and flicked on one of the dials, he casually inquired, "How do you plan to get there?"

"Howie is supposed to fly me out."

"I doubt that. He's not scheduled to come back until next week."

"Huh-unh. My brother made all of the arrangements. The

schedule says Howie will come back on Saturday."

Giving her a victorious smile, Ben shook his head. "Next Saturday, Cookie. Not tomorrow."

"No, that's not true. I have a schedule here someplace." She rifled through the diaper bag and plucked a sheet of paper from it. "Here we are. . . . Saturday. See?"

Shrugging at the paper, Ben didn't even bother to take the yellow memo from her. "Your brother blew it. Howie usually comes twice a week, but he can't return tomorrow or Tuesday on his usual route because he and the missus are celebrating their anniversary. Several of us pitched in and are sending them to Hawaii. He'll be back next Saturday. You're stuck here in the meantime."

Her heart leapt. *I get to stay with Troy for another week?* She stammered, "Impossible."

"No, it's merely inconvenient. Saddling me with a kid is impossible. You'll learn that soon enough. By the time Howie returns, you'll have come to that conclusion and take Troy back so he can have a decent, loving home." Ben turned and dumped a small, canvas sack out on the dining table. Leafing through the contents as his stew reheated, he waved an envelope in the air. "Guess what? I just got your letter. The zip code was wrong. It looks like it's been around a bit."

"At least that proves you're Troy's guardian."

"No, it doesn't. I'm not accepting this responsibility. It's absolute folly for me to take him on. I'm not set up for a baby. I take off for a week at a time to go hunting or fishing, Wendy. He won't get the love and attention he deserves, and I'm not about to let him grow up neglected just because my stepsister didn't think things through carefully."

Wendy lowered her gaze to her lap. She couldn't bear for him to see the longing in her eyes. The ache of wanting a baby burned in her heart. This wasn't about what she wanted, though. Her trip here was about duty and carrying out Laura's last wishes for her son. "Laura obviously thought you would be sufficiently caring."

"She hung onto fond memories of an older teenager who tolerated her during a few awkward years. That doesn't necessarily translate into making me father material. You can stay here, but you're seeing to him. I'm totally ignorant about babies, and I aim to stay that way."

Her heart leapt and beat an urgent rhythm against her ribs. *Would he let me keep Troy? No. It isn't right. Laura wanted Troy to go to him. Stop being selfish. Things'll work out. . . .* "Let's make a deal. I'll stay here with you for the week and teach you to care for Troy."

"I'm offering to have you stay as my house guest, to share my food, baby-sit him, enjoy my evening company." He paused strategically. "All in exchange for you taking him south when Howie comes back."

"That's blackmail!"

three

Ben shrugged. "Desperate men do desperate things."

"I want to use the phone."

"The phones are out. I have a radio."

"Please call my brother. I can't agree to your bargain, so he'll arrange for a charter pilot to come get me."

"We can try, but you won't have any luck. Abe Hunters is the only other pilot who flew this region, and he's down with a roaring case of hepatitis. Since both are out, you're stuck."

"Surely, there must be someone else. I read a lot of Alaskans own their own planes."

"Three of the families here do, but don't get your hopes up. The Seal twins are doing research and went to the polar ice cap for two weeks to get readings. The Perns' son borrowed their plane to take his boys on a trip, and Gil, Harry, and Cletus sent their plane to Anchorage for a complete overhaul and electrical work."

She gawked, then spluttered, "What if there were an emergency?"

"This isn't an emergency." He went on to admit, "Unless there's a medical emergency, no one's available to fly. Even then, it would still take time and loads of luck."

"This is horrible!"

Taking in her appalled expression, Ben managed to keep from grinning like the Cheshire cat. He offered magnanimously, "We can have the operator send a message to your boyfriend so he doesn't worry."

"I don't have anyone other than my brother." Her tone went strangely flat. Ripping the sling from her shoulder, she stated, "I'm exhausted."

"It's easy to see why."

"What was that crack supposed to mean?"

Her heated tone took him by surprise. Ben tilted his head to the side and mentally replayed the conversation. "Oh! I meant that it's easy to see why you're tired. I wasn't trying to taunt you about not having a boyfriend." The distressed look in her eyes made him wonder what had happened.

She bit her lip and nodded.

She changed moods and personalities so fast, he couldn't keep up with her. One minute, she was impish and mischievous, possessing a musical laughter that would charm any man. The next, she was ill-tempered as could be. Maybe she just needed some rest. "Go ahead and turn in."

"I will."

He shook his head, thinking of the narrow bed in the guest room. "What about the kid?"

She sighed. "Howie said there wasn't room on the plane for the crib. He'll bring it on another trip. In the meantime, you'll have to make do with the playpen."

"Me?" He shook his head. "Oh, no. I'm not handling him."

"Ben, I'm exhausted. I'll watch Troy during the daytime, and we'll share evening duty, but you have to handle him at night."

"I don't know what to do with a kid at night."

"You let him sleep." She winced, and her eyes took on a haunted look. "Most babies his age wake up maybe once a night, if at all. Unfortunately he's been upset by this upheaval, so he's been getting up a few times. When he wakes up, you feed him, burp him, and change him. You're able to perform all three of those skills." Her tone cracked as she tacked on, "That puts me out of the picture."

"Lady, you're really ticking me off."

"Frankly, Ben, I'm so tired, I'd probably sleep through most of your tirade. Unless you have something vitally important to say that won't keep until morning, I'm calling it quits. Drag the playpen out from the other room and let Troy sleep in it."

He looked at her critically. Dark crescents shadowed her eyes, and her features looked strained. Weariness made her shoulders droop. Traveling with a baby must have been a nightmare. "Okay. It'll keep. We have a week."

She stood and paused. "You owe me a nice, long shower."

He decided to tease her to lighten the tension vibrating between them. Pasting on a mock look of surprise and waggling his brows, he said in a shocked tone, "Miss Marbury!"

"That's not what I meant." She inched back a few steps. "I don't believe in permissive behavior. If you have any designs or desires, you'd better forget them here and now." The way the blood drained from her face and she put distance between them doubled the impact of her words.

"Wendy—"

She put up her hands as if to ward him off. "This was a bad idea. I'll just leave and stay with—"

"There isn't anywhere for you to go, and there's no need either," he said in a tone he hoped sounded both firm and reassuring. "Forgive me. My humor was tacky, but I didn't really mean anything by it. I made you uncomfortable, and I'm sorry. Just forget—"

"I need to stay elsewhere."

He folded his arms akimbo in exasperation. "There isn't anywhere else, Wendy."

She stuck out her hand. "Your car—give me the keys."

"You wouldn't know where you're going. You could get lost out there. You haven't even said where you're from, but I know you won't have an inkling of how to survive up here."

She waggled her fingers. "The keys."

"You're perfectly safe with me, Wendy."

"I'll go out and sleep in your car. The doors lock. During the daytime, when you're at work, I'll come in to take care of Troy. Give me the keys."

"Honey, I don't own a car. All I have is an ATV and a snowmobile. I'll just take a few diapers and some wipes from your bedroom and keep Troy out here in his playpen. There's a lock on the spare bedroom. You go on in there, bolt the door, and sleep. At this point, you're so tired, you're getting paranoid."

She kept her distance. "I can't believe this. They assured me you were set up and wanted Troy. Mr. Nagel insisted I had to bring him up right away, that you expected him. I was simply supposed to help settle him in and check in on you tomorrow before I left."

"We've been over this, Wendy. You're obviously exhausted from the long flight, and emotions are running high. I know it probably feels weird, having to share my cabin—"

She nodded emphatically.

"So we'll just keep focused on Troy. How does that sound?"

"If you can't, I'll bundle up and walk until I find shelter."

"Go to bed, Wendy. You're safe here. You have my word on it." He stepped back, watched her slip into the room, and frowned at the way she hurriedly shut the door between them. The lock clicked loudly, as if to punctuate her fright. Ben winced—he'd been out of line, and he'd scared the poor woman.

Why did he feel guilty? She'd appeared out of nowhere and tried to saddle him with a kid. He stared at her door.

Lord, regardless of how harebrained her scheme is, we're still stuck together for the next week. With Your help, I can manage. I don't want her afraid of me. We already have more than enough to cope with.

At a quarter after eleven, he heard Wendy pacing. A full hour passed before the bed squeaked and she fell silent. Not long thereafter, Troy woke up and hollered. Ben put down his fishing magazine, picked up the baby, and shoved a bottle into his grasping hands. Troy seemed less than thrilled with the offering. Ben coaxed him into taking all of two ounces, and he continued to whine and fuss until Ben was ready to do something drastic. He changed the diaper and couldn't figure out why the boy was still sounding off. As a matter of fact, his volume escalated to something akin to a civil defense disaster siren.

Wendy stumbled out of the room. She'd drawn a fluffy, dark green housecoat around herself and belted it shut with a knot that would do any sailor proud. Her long, flannel night-gown peeked out at the neck and hem.

"Thank heavens! It's about time you came and rescued us. What's his problem?"

She wearily checked things over for all of three seconds and gave him a dismayed look. "You took the bottle straight out of the refrigerator and didn't warm it up? He's got a tummy ache."

"How was I supposed to know to warm it up?" Ben snatched the bottle and strode to the kitchen.

She followed on his heels and pulled it out of the microwave. "Never, ever microwave baby food or formula. It can get hot spots and scald Troy."

"Do you have to make everything difficult?"

"Yes. I love giving you a rough time." She filled a saucepan with water and heated the bottle on the range. "I flew up here just to make your life miserable. Dumping orphans off on ill-tempered relatives is a specialty of mine."

"All right, I deserved that."

"It's freezing here."

"Amazing," he mocked. "You are in Alaska, you know."

"Don't remind me. I was hoping it was just all a bad dream." She drew in a deep breath. "I apologize. I'm snapping at you, and it's not right. I'm cold. Do you have any extra blankets?"

"Oh, sorry too," he said sheepishly. "I got so wrapped up with everything else, I didn't even think of that." He opened a closet and pulled out two thick, wool blankets.

"The bottle ought to be about ready. Test the formula on the inside of your wrist. If it's comfortably warm, it's fine."

"Then what do I do?" He handed the blankets to her.

"You have to burp him first. He's gulping air when he cries. Feed him, but stop halfway and burp him, and then do it again when he's done. Troy's got a finicky stomach. Most babies his age don't need to be burped, but he's miserable if you skip it. If he's still fussy, you'll need to strip him and let him be skin-to-skin with you so his belly relaxes."

"Wendy, I'm in no mood for jokes."

"I'm not joking. It helps."

"If I take his pants off, he'll wet all over me."

Her features tightened. "Leave the diaper on, Ben."

"That's a step in the right direction, but all of those steps are still too involved." He glanced at the clock and yawned. "Why can't he just sleep with you? You'd keep him warm, especially with these blankets, and I could finally get enough sleep so I'm not a zombie at work tomorrow."

"I've devoted my life to Troy this last month. While I'm here, I'll take care of him during the daytime, but I can't do it anymore—not at night when you're home."

Ben suspected she'd spoken part of the truth, but not all of it. He sensed she cared for Troy, and he needed her help with him. "I don't think a few more nights would make any difference."

"We have to let him get used to you. He'll still have me during the days when you work so he'll be able to transition all right, but a baby deserves undivided attention and love from the person who is going to rear him. Laura and Mike chose you, Ben. If you want to snuggle with Troy, that's fine with me."

"I'll roll over and turn him into a pancake."

"Then feed him and hope for the best." She hugged the blankets closer to her chest, as if to take the place of the little guy, and bowed her head momentarily. "I'm truly sorry this is so unexpected and difficult, Ben. I thought that you'd had advance warning, so it has to be a rude shock. Give yourself a chance to accept the situation and get used to Troy. He's a good little baby."

He took pains to be sure his voice wasn't querulous when he quietly asked, "Then why don't you keep him?"

Silence stretched between them. When she finally answered, her voice was equally muted, and sadness threaded through each word. "I can't. I work odd hours, and that won't ever change. The past four-and-a-half weeks of juggling both life and Troy took more than I had to give."

"I see."

"Do you?"

Her gaze locked with his, the green somehow darkened to a mossy color that made him realize her admission was actually painful. He caught his breath. Ben suspected much hadn't been said, and he wondered just how attached she'd grown to the baby during the past month.

"Yes, I think I do." He sighed. "I used the phone number printed in the lawyer's letter and made radio contact with a friend who called your brother. Your brother wasn't there, but we left a message to warn him you won't make it home 'til next week."

She granted him an unbelievably sweet smile. "Thank you, Ben. I appreciate your thoughtfulness."

His heart softened even more. This woman was special. She'd given four-and-one-half weeks to a baby and made this trip. Obviously exhausted, she still had it in her to summon up gratitude. "You're practically asleep on your feet. Go on to bed."

"Gladly."

"If he, uh—" Ben hedged. "I mean, well. . .I'll get you if Troy doesn't calm down."

"Please don't. I'm sure you can take care of his needs." She stumbled back to her bedroom and shut the door. Again, the lock clicked.

Ben frowned down at Troy. "You know, Buster, I'm not sure what's worse—you being noisy, or her being scared of me. I don't know how to fix either problem. Good thing this is just a temporary situation."

Twenty minutes later, Ben knocked on that same door. Wendy didn't answer, so he tried again. When she didn't respond, he called her name through the door. Troy was still pitching a royal fit. At wit's end, Ben wasn't ashamed to demand help even if she'd pled so pitifully for him to leave her in peace. He'd done his best, and this strange woman was undeniably skilled with Troy. Finally, he banged on the door and shouted, "Wendy, you've gotta help me."

She barely opened the door a crack.

"I can't get him to settle down."

Wendy rested her forehead against the edge of the door and closed her eyes. "Give me a minute," she mumbled. "I'll be out."

Ben stepped back and impatiently paced across the living room floor a few times. Troy's wails continued. Relief flooded Ben when Wendy shuffled out in her robe, carrying a blanket.

It seemed as if she moved in slow motion. Her steps lagged, and the ivory blanket dragged along the floor beside her like a bridal train gone awry.

She moaned softly as she sat on the couch, then seemed to have far too much difficulty lying down and rolling onto her side. Cold did that to some folks—made them stiff. She must be one of them. Ben watched and felt a twinge of remorse for the sacrifice he asked of her. According to what he'd gathered, she'd given too much of herself to this matter in the last month. That was a long time, an eternity. One evening, and he was ready to cash in his chips.

Troy's racket escalated.

"Wendy—"

She half yawned, half sighed. "Give him here." After wriggling a bit more, she accepted Troy, stuffed him under the blanket, and cuddled him in the curve of her body while supporting him with her arm. She drew him close, and he burrowed into her warmth. Troy's bellows lessened in volume. Patting him and rubbing his back in a slow rhythm, she began to hum softly.

"Here," Ben whispered, slipping the blanket up to her neck.

"Don't you dare disappear. Once he's asleep, you have to take him back."

"Don't be so coldhearted. He's finally calming down and clamming up. Let us all get some sleep, will you?"

"This couch isn't safe for both of us."

"Then let me carry him into your bedroom."

She gave him a jaded look. "The twin bed isn't wide enough to be safe."

"Then I'll sleep here. You and the baby can take my bed."

"No."

"Wendy—"

"No."

"It would be for the best—"

"No."

"For all of us. We need to get some sleep."

"I said no!"

In spite of their battle, Troy started to relax. He let out several hiccuping breaths and began to settle down. Her rubbing continued. Now, she resumed humming.

"I have to go to the bathroom."

"You'd better come back in three minutes, or I'm going to do something drastic."

"You can't do anything more nightmarish than giving me custody of an infant. Your threat holds no substance." Ben turned off the light, walked away, and intentionally stayed out for a fair chunk of time. When he eventually returned, it was only because there wasn't a single sound coming from the living room. He figured he'd be safe to tell her that she and Troy had both fallen asleep and he didn't want to disturb them.

Truthfully, they were both asleep. To pull them apart seemed unnatural. The way she cradled little Troy against her warmth looked unspeakably tender. Then again, she'd practically begged Ben to let her have time alone before he'd foisted his nephew upon her. Ben couldn't figure her out. Her speech and actions didn't match up.

Okay, he could understand why she didn't want Troy to sleep with her. Although the baby seemed satisfied, that position admittedly couldn't be half as comfortable for Wendy.

She'd voiced the opinion that it wouldn't be safe for both of them to share the narrow sofa. She'd been concerned the twin mattress wasn't wide enough either. It would be foolishly absurd, if not downright dangerous, to leave Troy with her.

Uncomfortable with that entire line of thinking, Ben shifted his weight from one foot to the other. His body moved just enough to let in more light from the hall. A shaft of light hit her cheek, and he felt his heart do a sickening lurch. She'd fallen asleep, all right; but tears still glistened on her cheeks, making it clear exhaustion became her refuge instead of her enemy.

four

Guilt pressed in on Ben. He knew Wendy was tired, but he hadn't realized she was that tired. For a woman to cry at all bothered him, but for her to cry herself to sleep made his heart clench. He gently smoothed several wild curls away from her cheek. Though not stunningly beautiful by any stretch of the imagination, she certainly rated far above what he'd consider average. There was something engaging about her. Probably her eyes, he decided. She had exquisite eyes. They flashed with both humor and anger. Now that they were closed, he discovered a softness, a vulnerability to her he hadn't noticed earlier.

"Why couldn't you just be a housekeeper, Cookie?" he whispered softly. "Until the baby started to cry, I thought maybe heaven had smiled on me and sent you here. You'd be the answer to a lonely man's prayers. As selfish as it sounds, I have to admit that I want you all to myself. Over the last year, I finally decided God might be able to work a miracle in my heart someday and give me a woman to love forever, but He knows I'm not made to be a father."

The room remained silent except for the soft snuffles coming from the bundle cuddled to her breast and the slow, deep breaths Wendy took. Ben had to admit she looked fulfilled when she curled around that baby. . .as if she might have been her very own. In the moments when she'd helped by holding Troy, she'd had the sweetest smile on her face. Mothering came to her as naturally as breathing.

He'd never seen a woman look as completely satisfied as she did just holding this child. His fantasy was just that—a fantasy. Wendy Marbury might not have a kid of her own, but she was a mother at heart. He could forget considering her as anything more, because she would want marriage and little ones, and he wasn't a family man. Yes, he could probably find a lot of joy in marriage, but he simply didn't see himself ever putting up with children.

As Ben watched, Troy squirmed. Wendy automatically shifted and cuddled the baby. Yes, she dipped her head; but did she press a kiss on Troy's downy head, or simply reposition herself since the pillow had slipped away? Ben scanned the width of the couch and knew if Troy flipped over, he'd be right on the floor. There was no way around it—Ben had to take him back to the playpen.

Trying hard to move quietly and keep Troy asleep, Ben slid his hands under the blanket and took possession of the baby. A pocket of heat surrounded his little body. The back of Ben's hand inadvertently brushed against the sleeve of Wendy's fluffy robe, and a wave of warmth enveloped him.

The soft nap of the heavy fabric reminded him of all he'd come to Alaska to avoid. He enjoyed the sound of women's laughter, the smell of their perfume, the way they livened up, yet gentled a man's world—but he'd come here because he loved being self-sufficient. Living the rugged life and enjoying solitude made Alaska perfect for him, but women were inherently social creatures. He'd never met a woman who would gladly give up the whirl and excitement of city living for a Klondike cabin. Differences would tear them apart, and he didn't believe in divorce, so he'd come up here and made a good life for himself. Yet here temptation lay in the form of a spirited woman. The one brief kiss he'd pressed on her cheek was enough to whet his appetite for more.

Ben jerked back. "The baby," he told himself. "I'll just take care of the baby for a little while. That ought to cure me of this." Trying to ignore his immediate and overwhelming response to the woman, he lifted Troy out. He thought to tuck the tyke into his own shirt to make up for the loss of Wendy's incubator-like comfort.

Her eyes drifted half open, and she made a small, distressed sound as the baby's absence registered.

"Shh. I have the little guy. I know you wanted a locked door between us, but with the heater vents sealed off, that room got impossibly cold. You can't sleep in there. I have fresh sheets on my bed. Go on in—"

"Unh-unh. Fine here. . ." Her voice faded off.

Ben sighed. Arguing with her wouldn't accomplish a thing other than to upset her more. "Go on back to sleep." He juggled Troy in one arm and started to cover Wendy again. She let out a shattered sigh, rolled away, and whimpered. That sound bothered him. "Wendy, you're safe here. I promise—you don't have to be afraid of me."

She huddled more tightly and whispered something unintelligible.

Her room was beyond chilly. He decided to leave the door open. He'd sealed off the vent to prevent wasting heating oil. Since he normally used the room only to work out, he stayed warm enough without the heat. Scanning the floor, he absently wondered how she'd managed to stack all of his stuff neatly off to the side and fit the baby's junk in here too. Since it didn't much matter at the moment, he walked away and popped Troy into the playpen he'd put in the corner of his room.

Just in case she got cold, Ben tiptoed back out to the living room and carefully draped two more covers on Wendy. He slipped back into his bedroom and discovered Troy had kicked off his blanket. As Ben tucked the satin-edged softie back up on the baby, he snorted in disbelief. He was fussing over a woman and a kid like a leg-shackled husband!

&

Troy's crying awakened Wendy. It quickly rose to insistent, loud bawling. For an instant she tried to figure out where she was. Reality hit, and she bit back a moan of despair.

The crying escalated to a nearly hysterical pitch.

She threw back the covers and sucked in an alarmed breath. It was cold! Wendy padded toward the noise and plucked an outraged Troy from the playpen. "What's the matter, Buddy?"

He grabbed a fistful of her robe, closed his eyes, and wailed some more.

"Hungry, lonely, and wet," she decided. "Ben?" When he gave no response, she noted that the laundry room and bathroom doors were open. His bed was made and there was no sign of his presence at all. A terse note lay on the dining table: "I get home at four thirty."

ॐ

Ben got home at six. Wendy sat at the table. "You're late."

"Give me a break. We had a problem at work. The phone is still out so I couldn't call." Irritated, he grumbled, "I don't feel like listening to you complain because you were here all day with Troy, because that is exactly what you're doing—trying to strand me with that kid."

She set down her fork. Her voice went low and shaky. "I didn't ask to be a part of this any more than you did. He's not my relative."

"He's not mine either. He's my stepsister's kid—what does that make me? A stepuncle? Give me a break!"

"That's more than I am. I'm nothing."

The raw emotion in her words silenced him. He paused and considered what to do. He needed her help with the baby until Howie got back, and with every passing moment, he became more sure she'd grown attached to Troy and was torn by the whole situation. He needed to calm down and diffuse the tension. Maybe then she wouldn't be so jumpy and defensive.

"Look, Wendy," he said in a carefully modulated tone, "this conversation isn't getting us anywhere."

"I agree. Are you off tomorrow?"

"I work for the next five days." The look of disbelief on her face made him hasten to add, "Jim and I traded days off so I could go hunting earlier in the month, and he's off doing the same now."

She let out a despondent breath, then smoothed back a few stray curls. "We'll have to use the evenings to transition Troy into your care."

"I have a couple of days to decide what to do. We can just get through the next week like we did today." His eyes widened as he looked at the coffee table. The haphazard stack of magazines that usually topped it was missing. Instead, a blanket, wipes, diapers, and a battered tube of diaper rash ointment adorned it. "What happened around here? What have you done to my coffee table?"

"It's the changing table now."

"Oh, no, it's not. This is my home, not a nursery school, and you and that baby are a temporary blight on my kingdom, nothing more!"

She gave him a wounded look and pressed her lips together.

I'm not going to let her make me feel guilty.

She looked down at the table and picked up her knife and fork.

I'm not going to let her make me feel guilty.

The second she lifted a bite to her mouth, he became aware of the mouth-watering aroma that filled the cabin.

Whoa. She watched the kid all day and made supper, and I came home and yelled. Now I feel guilty—but not guilty enough to lose my appetite.

"What are we having?" Ben hastily stepped past the diaper-stacked coffee table and reached her side.

"I don't know. None of that meat in the freezer is labeled."

Ben practically drooled as he stared at her plate. The succulent-looking meat, a baked potato, and small serving of colorful mixed vegetables looked like something from a TV ad or magazine spread. A glance at the rest of the table made his jaw go tight. She'd set it for one. He growled her name angrily.

She started to rise. "What?"

He cast a hasty glance at the stove as a last ditch hope, but the pots were empty. "It wouldn't have been any more trouble to make me some."

"But—"

He yanked open the refrigerator and ignored her splutters. "Don't even bother to make an excuse."

"Fine." She sat down and made a show of cutting a bite of the succulent-looking meat as he gave up on locating anything vaguely edible in the fridge. Steam curled over her plate, carrying more of the mouth-watering aroma.

Now I know why Esau sold his birthright. That food is enough to make a hungry man act like a fool. He cleared his throat. "I told you that there's plenty of food in the attic."

"I don't know how to get up into the attic, and what about the baby? If I were to get stuck up there or fall, it would be disastrous."

She had a point. The attic access was a simple pull-down hatch, but he'd artfully concealed it into the laundry room ceiling. He doubted that she could even reach the latch.

"Forget it. I'll find something." He rifled through the cabinets and had to admit the cabinets looked essentially bare. The notable exceptions were the shelf with a set of dinky bottles of herbs and spices he didn't know how to use and another shelf upon which she'd stacked an impressive supply of jarred baby food and cans of formula. He'd bought the collections of spices on a whim last year, but they never saw the light of day. Ignoring them, he took a jar of baby food, read the label, and reviewed the contents. He thrust the jar toward Wendy so she could verify its existence. "I'll just eat these baby Vienna sausages."

"Be my guest."

"Thanks, I will." Just to spite her and make her feel bad, he got out a plate and dumped the tiny hot dogs onto it. He even microwaved them for a short while to drive home his point. After putting his napkin in his lap, he stabbed one with his fork and remarked, "Hot dogs are hot dogs. If you want to be selfish, fine. I can still manage to scrape together something decent to eat."

Wendy just looked at him.

Ben popped the little wiener into his mouth, chewed once, and stopped cold. He yanked up his napkin and emptied his mouth at once.

"Enjoying your decent meal?" She smiled at him with owl-eyed innocence.

"Someone ought to be shot for labeling that as food!"

"Oh, really? Aren't you the man who just declared I was selfish and he could manage on his own?"

"Okay, so I was wrong."

"For that, I'll take pity." She wiped her mouth, got up, and pulled a plate from the oven. It held a generous portion of meat and a huge potato. Vegetables and a leftover roll also perched there. After setting the meal down in front of an astonished Ben, she slipped back in her seat.

Ben didn't hesitate for a second. He dug in at once. "I guess I owe you an apology."

"I held dinner for awhile, but Troy went to sleep, and you still hadn't come home. I decided to eat while I had a moment of peace and quiet."

Ben chuckled self-consciously. "So much for peace and quiet. I shattered both."

"I know I've upset you by bringing Troy, and you don't know me at all. Still, if we could try to give each other the benefit of the doubt, things might go better."

"You're right. I'm edgy about this whole baby thing, but being nasty won't help." He shot her a boyish grin. "I know there's a proverb about a meal of herbs served with love is better than a feast in a home filled with strife. You made a feast, so I'll cut the strife. This is incredible. What is it?"

"I don't know. Call it Anonymous Alaskan." Her hair fell like a privacy curtain between them.

Tenderly, he tucked her soft tresses behind her ear. "Hey." When she kept her head bowed, he lifted her chin and studied her features. Her cheeks had gone pale, and emotion darkened the color of her glistening eyes to a deep moss. He caught his breath. "Wendy?"

Her shoulder hitched in a gesture that didn't seem quite as blasé as she probably hoped it did. "I hoped Troy would fill your home with love."

"Since we're all stuck together for the next week, why don't we declare a truce?"

"Okay," she rasped as she stood.

"Where are you going?" A squeak from the other room answered his question.

A few moments later, Wendy returned with Troy. She'd wrapped him in a satin-edged flannel blanket. The stupid thing had purple bunnies hopping across every inch.

"It doesn't look like you got to finish your meal without both of us interrupting you." The minute the words slipped out, Ben regretted them. He winced as he thought aloud, "That's what you meant last night, wasn't it—about Troy taking more than you had to give. Every time you turn around, you have to stop what you need to do to take care of him."

Again, her eyes darkened with emotion. Instead of confirming his suspicion, she rasped, "Your supper is going to get cold."

"So will yours, Cookie." He pulled her plate closer and proceeded to cut her meat. "Here. Eat. We'll finish supper, then I'll watch the kid so you can take a shower."

She cleared her throat. "Thank you. That sounds good."

An hour later, Ben stared at Wendy as she emerged from the shower. They'd eaten a reheated supper, then she'd silently slipped away. Her hair, though damp, already sported bouncy curls. "You washed your hair too? You were in there for all of twelve minutes!"

She shrugged nonchalantly. "I've gotten used to taking quick ones. Guardians don't have much time to themselves."

"I thought about cleaning up the kitchen, but I couldn't. I had to watch the kid. How did you manage to make supper with him under foot?"

"It isn't easy. Come on into the kitchen. I'll show you how to fix Troy's bottles for the night."

"How about if I change him and let you take care of that?"

"I might take you up on that offer in a few days, but right now, you have to learn how to take care of his needs."

"No, I don't. You're here. You do an excellent job."

"We both know I'll be gone in six days."

"So will Troy."

"Ben, I'm not in a mood to fight with you. Please try to learn. Give it an honest effort. Even if you really decide to place Troy in an adoptive home, you need to screen the prospective parents. You'll have to take care of him in the meantime."

"I don't need to do that. I've already decided whom I'll give him to."

"You have?"

"Yes. You."

five

"Mc!"

Ben nodded emphatically. "I'm determined to assign you as his guardian."

Hope flared. Wendy stared at him, temporarily overwhelmed by the fact that he'd just made her dream come true. Troy would be hers! Never in all the days she'd held him had Wendy allowed herself to believe Troy might truly be her very own. Oh, she'd fantasized, but enough reality intruded to keep her from letting hope overtake her. Separating would be heart-wrenching enough without setting herself up for total devastation.

"I'm serious," Ben went on. "You're terrific with him, and he's used to you."

Her legs went limp. Wendy slumped and tumbled backward onto the couch. With that jolt, reality flooded back. She could barely take care of herself. They had no place to live other than with her brother. Between paying off loans and shelling out money for child care, she'd barely afforded diapers for Troy. His parents were poor as Job's turkey, so he'd inherited virtually nothing. Even if she paid off her last loan and started receiving Social Security for Troy, it would be a year or more before she could responsibly provide for a baby and manage motherhood.

The bitter taste of defeat flooded her mouth and tainted her heartbeat. Each breath stung as she struggled to keep from weeping. How dare he so blithely give away all she wanted so desperately?

"You. . .you've taken leave of your senses!"

"Not at all. I believe the plan has exceptional merit."

She drummed her fingers on the arm of the couch in

extreme agitation. How could he do this to her—offer her what she wanted more than anything in the world and knew she couldn't accept? She almost threw her arms around him and shouted her heartfelt thanks, until she remembered her situation. She was in no condition to provide for the boy. Yet Ben wore a resolute expression.

Wendy struggled to sound sincere. "Laura wanted you to rear him, Ben. I think I'd better call your attention to the very important fact that I haven't asked for him."

"Neither did I."

"Oh, for pity's sake, Ben! Troy's a nice kid, and he deserves your love. Stop being so selfish and accept him. He's yours, whether you wanted him or not. You aren't supposed to dump him off on someone else just because you don't think of your-self as Father of the Year."

"Hear me out. I'm exceptionally well paid and don't spend but a fraction of my salary. I can pay for you to have maid ser-vice and a part-time nanny. I'll be as generous as you ask."

"Money only takes care of part of the shortfall. Love and energy can't be bought." She cranked her head to the side to hide the tears stinging her eyes and the guilty look on her face. Everything in her heart cried out to accept the baby, but her head denied her.

"But you like him, don't you?"

Dear God, don't let him do this to me! Don't let him tempt me like this! "Forget trying to sweet-talk me, Ben." She drew a fortifying breath. "It won't work. I like plenty of things and people, but it doesn't mean that I fill my entire life with them. An arrangement like that isn't fair to anyone."

"I've seen you with him. I have every assurance you'd fall in love with him."

"So will you," she countered swiftly. For every excuse she gave, a part of her cried out in anguish. Why did he have to do this—dangle her most ardent hope before her when she knew full well this wasn't the way to settle such an important issue. He truthfully didn't know her from Eve, and he was going to happily pack off his legal ward without any hesitation. It alarmed her.

Ben shoved the diapers to the side and sat down on the coffee table. He leaned forward, propped his forearms above the knees of his well-washed jeans, and looked her in the eye.

"Wendy, I don't know how to get you to understand that I'm trying to do what's best for Troy. You don't know me. Honestly, I'm not a family man. I'm the quintessential bachelor. I haven't married because I'm just not interested in the family scene."

"You told me you're a Christian." Her voice turned into a strangled choke. "Surely, you're not. . ."

He threw back his head and nearly caused an avalanche with his raucous laughter. After he reestablished his composure, he gave her a thorough once-over that left her blushing clear down to her toes. "Believe me, Cookie, I'm as straight as straight can be."

She tried not to think about why that piece of news pleased her so much. For a moment, she was completely tongue-tied.

His eyes twinkled wickedly as he added, "Yep, straight as an arrow. . .a man who appreciates a pretty woman." His voice dropped register on the last few words, giving them added meaning.

Who ever called Alaska cold? Right about now, it was sizzling. Steaming. Wendy fought the impulse to fan herself. Ben twisted a few short phrases and let his eyes roam in such a way that her thoughts suddenly soared to the very boundary of decency—and from the seductive smile on his face, she realized it too.

She knew she'd better snap out of it and keep to the subject about the baby. *Keep your thoughts, words, and heart pure and pleasing to God, Wendy.* After clearing her throat, she rasped, "We need to limit ourselves to discussing Troy's welfare and care."

To his dismay, Ben realized she was sticking to business. He'd best stay with it too. Ben clamped a lid on his hormones and rubbed a hand across his jaw. Wendy didn't act flirtatious like other women he'd known, and her modesty made him realize he far preferred her style. Steering his thoughts away from her and onto the baby would be a smart move—for both of them. "Okay, let's focus on the boy's needs. Since I'm such a bachelor I haven't even managed to hook up with a wife— who would have to be fairly self-sufficient," he added on in a pointed tone. "How can I be committed to a baby who needs everything done for him?"

"I can't answer that. What I do know is, he's yours right now. You owe it to Troy and to yourself to care for him to the very best of your ability. For you to try to avoid that or foist him off on me is wrong."

Her words rang with truth, even if he didn't particularly want to hear them. Ben stared silently at the baby. Troy rolled onto his side and stuffed his thumb in his mouth.

Wendy took in the sight too. Softening her voice, she suggested, "Make a vow that you'll do everything you can for him while I'm here. Give it your best effort. If you truly can't, then you'll have a clear conscience when you relinquish him."

"And when I relinquish him?"

"If you decide to relinquish him, I'll help you find someone who will cherish him, but you have to really put yourself out to earn my help." *If it really doesn't work for him, I'll see if he's sincere about helping out, because then, I could truly have Troy—but I can't tell him that. Not yet.*

"That's fair enough."

She stood up. "I guess you'd better learn how to make formula."

He sighed theatrically. "Shoved aside for a smelly little crybaby! My ego will never be the same."

"Maybe you ought to hit the bottle." She handed him one of Troy's bottles.

He chuckled as he followed her into the kitchen. Mixing formula didn't look so hard after all. He watched her demonstration, then measured out the powder, added the water, and shook. "How many do I make?"

"That's how you make one. It's far quicker to make eight at a time. I used a big pitcher and hand-held blender back home."

"Blender," he mused. Ben turned, scanned the cupboards, and opened one over the range. "I have one of those up here somewhere. . . . Here!" He pulled out a small appliance and proudly set it on the counter in front of her. "I used it to make milkshakes."

"Milkshakes?" She laughed in disbelief. "In Alaska?"

He gave her a mock frown. "You drink ice water, ice tea, and slushies. Ice belongs to Alaska."

"Well." She tugged at the waist of her sweatshirt and nodded as if making a big concession, "I thank you and all Alaskans for being big enough to share ice with the world."

"I can see you're humoring me. I'm not going to settle for your capitulation just because you're feeling charitable." He paused as though his words would be momentous, then cleared his throat and announced, "We are responsible for Baked Alaska!"

"Now that's worth a whole lot in my book."

A smirk tilted his lips. "Want to give me an award? I'll let you seal it with a kiss."

"Uh, I think I'll have to pass."

He sighed, then picked up a baby bottle. "Much more time around you, and I'm going to start hitting the bottle." As she giggled, he said, "You never said how many per day."

"He eats baby food three times a day and has about eight bottles besides. It's easiest if you make all of the bottles at once and set aside the jars so you make sure he has a balanced variety."

"Okay." He opened another cabinet. "Let's see. . .turkey and noodles, carrots, and pears. How does that sound?"

"I wasn't specific enough. I give him both a main dish and veggies for lunch and supper, just fruit and rice cereal or oatmeal for breakfast, and juice once a day."

He set out a few more jars and gestured at them. "What do you think?"

"You're missing the fruit."

"I hadn't thought of it that way. How about if we give him something sweet? Ah! Peaches."

She gave him a gamine smile and confessed, "Peaches are my favorite."

"You've eaten baby food?"

She giggled delightedly. "So have you."

He turned slightly green. "Don't remind me. Those things were awful."

"I know. Troy loves them, though. He zeros out the jar in nothing flat. You might want to remember that as a trick. On days when you're pressed for time or super tired, he can feed himself those instead of you spooning in the other stuff."

"Then that would be today. I'm about dead on my feet. If you don't mind, I'm going to shower and hit the hay. He got me up twice last night."

❧

Wendy didn't have the heart to remind Ben she'd told him to expect the same schedule until Troy felt more secure. He could discover that on his own.

Ben didn't discover it. He simply didn't wake up. Troy screeched at decibel levels rivaling acid rock concerts. Ben didn't even stir.

Unable to stand it, Wendy tried to wake him up, but to no avail. She even tried putting Troy in bed with him, but Ben blissfully rolled over and began to snore. She almost choked the next morning when she found his note. It joyously exclaimed, "He slept through the night!"

He must have scribbled the note in a hurry. His handwriting slanted upward in a broad scrawl. He'd propped the note against a backpack and added, "I wanted to get some food down from the attic, but I overslept—sorry. Hope you can find something here to tide you over."

Clearly, this was a camping supply. Individual servings of

dehydrated stew, mac and cheese, chili, half a bag of marsh-mallows, some nuts, and a few banged-up envelopes of hot chocolate promised she wouldn't starve.

As Wendy held the note, a knock on the front door made her jump. She looked down at her robe and nightgown and quavered, "Who is it?"

"Susan and Betty," a woman said as she pushed open the door. The two of them came on in, quickly shut the door, then peeled out of heavy jackets. "I'm Susan Blossom," said a short, round woman.

"Betty Packard," said the other. "And yes, we're sisters, so you'll probably mix us up. We wanted to come visit you and the baby."

Wendy laughed self-consciously. "I'm glad for the company. Sorry, I'm not dressed yet."

Betty trundled across the room and scooped up Troy. "Don't worry about it. When my children were this little, more often than not, I didn't get dressed 'til noon."

The ladies said they'd already had breakfast—a fact for which Wendy whispered a prayer of thanks since she had no idea what she'd fix with the cupboards looking as bare as Mother Hubbard's. Somehow, stew or chili didn't sound like morning menu items. She hastily changed into jeans, then served coffee.

After about an hour, Betty sighed, "I need to get back home and look at order forms. We run a hunting/photography tour business, and I need to gear up for the spring."

Susan bobbed her head in agreement. "I have plenty to do too." She smiled at Wendy. "If you ever decide California isn't for you, I think you'd do well up here. You're friendly, and all of the guys who unloaded your stuff said you're a real babe. Want me to do some matchmaking?"

Wendy had no problem producing a merry laugh at the outrageous offer. "Some of my friends back home teased me about doing some husband-hunting while I was up here, but I'll have to pass on that offer."

"We have lots of single men—nice ones."

As if I'd even bother to look at any of them after I've seen Ben. Oh, man, I need to get my head examined! I've got to get out of here before I do something else really stupid. Wendy shook her head. "Thanks, Susan, but I'm only here 'til the next flight out."

❧

When Ben got home, he saw Troy on the baby blanket on the floor and remembered suppertime last night when he'd laid there, happily chewing on the head of a plastic giraffe. The memory made him smile. His smile changed to a look of regret when he glanced at the couch.

Wendy lay on the couch, fast asleep. He could barely straighten his frame out across the cushions; she scarcely took up two of them. A white pocket Bible teetered on the edge of the sofa, and he hoped she'd found words of wisdom and comfort before drifting off. Even in her sleep, she had one arm trailing off the cushions so her fingers brushed Troy's blanket.

Ben tiptoed across the room and stood over Troy. The little boy gurgled and kicked delightedly when he spied his uncle. Ben couldn't help grinning back. He was a cute kid, after all. "Shhh," he whispered as he carefully lifted the boy and snuggled him on his shoulder. "Let the poor woman sleep a bit."

A short while later, Wendy opened her eyes and gasped.

"Hi! Troy's in the playpen, so stop worrying. Did you have a nice nap?"

"You're home." Her voice sounded husky and shy. She slowly rose and straightened out her clothes as she watched Ben put supper on the table.

He resisted making a witty retort and merely commented, "I tried to be quiet so you could sleep."

"The impossible dream," she quipped.

He pulled a pan out of the oven and exclaimed with obvious delight, "Meatloaf!"

"Mooseloaf. I hope I did okay with the seasoning. I've

never cooked moose before."

Ben inhaled the aroma. His eyes closed in ecstasy. When he opened them again, he smiled at her. "If it tastes half as good as it smells, I'm not going to complain."

"And if it tastes bad?"

"We'll feed it to Troy. After all, he likes those abominable wieners."

"He only has four teeth. You're going to have to stick with baby stuff for awhile yet. He's about due for his lamb and carrots." She walked into the kitchen and got a fancy gelatin salad out of the refrigerator.

Ben looked at the marshmallows and nuts in it. Why did women think to add bits and pieces to ordinary stuff to dress it up? He'd forgotten about doing so, but the salad looked far more appetizing. "That's tempting. Does Troy get some too?"

"No, he could choke on the nuts. You don't give kids under the age of three anything tiny like that. No nuts, jelly beans, marbles—you get the idea. You'll have to feed him his regular baby stuff."

"You didn't save the pears for me to feed him?"

"Was I supposed to?"

"I thought maybe you'd take pity and not have me shovel anything too obnoxious into him. I have a distinctly unpleasant memory of my aunt having me sample smooshed up beets to convince my baby cousin that they tasted delicious. To this day, I won't eat beets!"

Wendy sketched a halfhearted smile and started to slice the mooseloaf. Her moves were sure, but lacked the grace she'd exhibited at other times. Ben absently read the labels on the baby food. "This stuff doesn't look very appetizing."

She shrugged.

"Bet it smells nasty too."

Wendy made a noncommittal sound and continued to work.

"Formula isn't exactly a gourmet milkshake either. No wonder babies cry. They're complaining about the chow. How long does he have to eat this stuff?"

"A year for formula. The labels on the jars suggest age ranges."

When she opened the cupboard, he changed subjects. "I know there's hardly anything in the cabinets. I'll bring food down from the attic tonight."

She nodded. As she put the food on the table and poured coffee, she remained distant. He finally rested his hands on the counter and asked softly, "When are you going to look at me?"

"I beg your pardon?" She looked up as far as his chin.

"You're still doing it. You're avoiding my eyes, and I think it's a pity. There's nothing for you to be shy or embarrassed about. You rejected my plan to give Troy to you, but everything you do practically screams that you were made to be a mother."

Her feelings were raw, and her voice reflected it. "I'm not his mother!"

"We both know that. All I'm saying is, there's no shame in loving him."

Her eyes finally met his. She asserted firmly, "I know."

He smiled. "Good, then we agree that you no longer have to hold back your attention."

"I didn't agree to that at all!"

"Yes, you did." He took the coffee mugs and set them on the table. The meal smelled and looked tantalizing. "You really know your way around a kitchen. If you weren't so disapproving, I'd propose that you go south, ditch little Troy, and come back to be my cook. I still can't help but feel a tinge of disappointment. I thought I'd finally gotten lucky."

Wendy slid into her place at the table and stared at him. Her heart ached and voice cracked. "You did get lucky. You got Troy. He's a wonderful little boy."

"I'm sure he is. That was never the issue."

"What is the issue?"

Ben looked her straight in the eye. "My ability or capacity to parent. It's nonexistent."

"No, it's just dormant. It needs to be fostered and cultivated."

"The only thing I'm cultivating tonight is your promise

that I can have meatloaf sandwiches in my lunch tomorrow. This is dynamite!"

"We'll talk over the possibilities after you've fed and bathed Troy."

"Bathed him?" he rasped weakly.

"Yes, bathe him—as in dunk him in water to clean him up. He gets a bath every day."

"I thought maybe they just crawled through a car wash once a month."

"In case you hadn't noticed, he's not crawling yet. He'll do that pretty soon. He started something new today. He gets up on all fours and rocks back and forth. You'll need to get the childproof locks and install them on everything right away."

"That's pushing things," Ben clipped out abruptly.

"Instead of being mad at me, why can't you take it as a compliment that I think you'd be a good guardian? That first night, you told me you like a challenge. I can't think of any challenge more incredible than rearing a child. Think of this as an opportunity instead of a obligation."

"All I can think of is, I'm going to mess up his little life and twist his psyche. Kids deserve a real family—a mother and a father."

Wendy sucked in a pained breath.

His hand shot out and captured hers. He squeezed her hand gently and softened his voice. "I'm sorry. Some women are happy being on their own, but you strike me as someone who'd rather be with someone. You're too caring to be alone. Since I can't imagine men would ever ignore you, I figure that you're getting over a relationship."

The question in his voice deserved an answer. Wendy looked away. In a muted voice, she said, "My fiancé broke our engagement."

Ben turned her face back to his, stared directly into her eyes, and said succinctly, "The man was a fool."

Just as she opened her mouth to reply, something hit the door. The loud noise barely registered before the door swung wide open. A parka-clad, bearded man stomped his feet and came in. "Ben!"

Another, shorter, down-bundled man followed behind him. The sounds of another snowmobile warned of further interruption and drowned out his greeting.

"Harry, Cletus—what're you doing here?"

"Don't tell us you forgot." The door slammed shut. Both men stared at Wendy as they threw back the fur-lined parka hoods and opened their jacket fronts to reveal plaid wool shirts.

"It's poker night," the first one declared.

"Hey," the second one sniffed, "you actually have decent grub for us this time?"

Wendy turned to Ben and gave him an accusing glare. He looked completely baffled, so she said nothing. *What is it up here? Four visitors in one day? I wouldn't have that many in a week at home!*

Another thump on the door announced the other cohort. "That must be Gil," Ben muttered.

Cletus opened the door and yanked in a tall, thin man. Wendy marveled anyone could wear such heavy clothing and still look so lean. As Cletus slammed the door with a resounding bang, Troy startled and began to whimper.

Tempted to turn and walk straight out that same door, Wendy took a split second to decide whether to grab dinner and dash to the privacy of her room and leave Ben to his buddies and the baby, or perhaps she could—

"Ma'am," Gil said in a deep bass that managed to sound incredibly bashful. She glanced up and noted how he'd blushed until his ears went scarlet. "We heard Ben had a woman and baby."

Ben had a woman! She almost choked. What kind of gossip was circulating in Caribou Crossing? Great—the arctic had an overactive jungle line.

"Didn't believe it, though," Harry boomed as he jabbed Ben in the ribs with his elbow. "You with a foxy chick and a baby under your roof—who woulda guessed?"

Ben looked decidedly uncomfortable and unhappy as he performed introductions. His face went darker still as Cletus darted over to the table and inhaled deeply. Wendy stifled a giggle. She knew exactly what Ben was thinking: There go my mooseloaf sandwiches!

"Looks like we hit the jackpot," Cletus announced as he pulled out a chair and plopped into it.

Troy let out another sharp cry. Wendy turned, snatched him from the playpen, and got ready to shove him into Ben's arms. To her surprise, Gil stepped between them. "I'll take the little guy."

She hesitated.

A pained expression flitted across his features. "You can trust me. I know how to handle babies."

The room went strangely silent for a second. Wendy nodded and passed Troy over. Suddenly all of the men started to talk. Their tones sounded too jovial and hearty.

Something was up.

Wendy's heart lurched. Is Ben going to give Troy to this man? She trained her gaze on his left hand. No wedding band—but a lot of men don't wear rings. She wanted to tear Troy from his grasp and run.

"You're going to have to order diapers by the caseload, Ben," Gil said quietly.

The air exploded out of her lungs. Wendy hadn't realized she'd been holding her breath. Relief flooded her. Gil hefted Troy over his shoulder and silenced the baby's whimpers at once. Satisfied this man wasn't going to try to take Troy away from her and could safely handle him, she turned and wrapped her fingers around Ben's wrist. She dragged him off to the corner.

"It's not poker night!"

"Don't you think I know that?"

Relief caused his shoulders to slump. The taut lines around his mouth relaxed. "I don't even play poker. So now what do we do?"

"I'll cover the meat and put the platter in the oven so it stays warm. Do you have a box of instant potatoes in the attic?" All of the sudden, the whole situation struck her as sublimely ridiculous. She started to giggle. Ben gave her a strange look. "You're the only person I know who stores potatoes in the attic," she breathlessly explained.

"Yeah," he grinned. "It sounds weird, but I do have some up there."

"Okay. I need milk, potatoes, and a vegetable of some sort. Oh! Do you have some canned cherries?"

"Nope."

"Apples or peaches?"

"Undoubtedly."

She spun him around and gave his broad back a shove. "Don't just stand there—Hurry!"

Cletus's face fell as Wendy snatched the mooseloaf from the table. She felt a pang of guilt and explained, "I need to keep this warm 'til everything else is ready."

"Oh." His face lit up like Troy's when he got to wear the squeaky train bib. Wendy muffled another giggle. She glanced down and saw how Cletus casually set his hand on the table and kept a proprietary thumb on the edge of the plate holding the gelatin salad. Even her fake cough didn't quite camouflage the sound of her laughter.

After snapping off foil and covering the meat, Wendy jerked open the cupboards and worked like a wild woman. She added bouillon powder to the mooseloaf drippings, tossed in seasonings, and made gravy as water boiled for the instant potatoes.

"Harry!" Ben called from the attic. "Heads up!" Seconds later, the men formed a line to toss cans and boxes of food from the attic, to the living room, to the kitchen. Cletus reluctantly left the gelatin salad and started a patter going that made it sound like he was announcing a football game.

Wendy slipped past him, caught the potatoes, and hollered, "Interception!"

"Harry, be careful!" Ben roared from the attic. "Don't you dare bean her with the groceries."

Wendy laughed. "I haven't gotten any beans yet."

A few minutes later, Ben stood behind her. His hands bracketed her in place by holding the counter on either side of her. He peered over her shoulder. "Are you okay?"

"Sure. Why?" She turned a bit and wished she hadn't. He was way too close. With his head dipped like that, their lips almost touched. She drew in a silent gasp.

Ben stared at her surprise-parted lips. He wished the guys weren't here. He'd gladly press his lips to her and take full advantage of their proximity. She'd taste so sweet, just like her scent. The woman wore the most incredible perfume. Months of being without a woman sensitized a man to the smallest of details, and he'd nearly gone wild just being close enough to inhale her scent these last few days. He wanted to drink it in.

"What is it?" she asked, nervously rubbing at her nose.

He reached out and brushed a tiny speck of flour from her cheek. *Her skin is so soft. . .soft as Troy's.* He mentally shook himself. Her wide green eyes carried more than a hint of wariness. He cleared his throat, then rasped, "Are you sure they didn't conk you on the head?"

"No."

His hand slid through her soft brown curls. They looped around his fingers, ensnared him. "No, you're not sure; or no, they didn't whack you?"

"No, I didn't get knocked in the noggin."

He let go and forced himself to draw farther away. "You're mixing chunks of butter with dry oatmeal, and you put eggshells with the coffee beans."

"I know what I'm doing."

He gave her a dubious look.

"Go set three more places at the table." As she slipped past him, Wendy brushed his arm, and that innocent contact nearly reduced him to cinders. He'd always appreciated women, but he'd never let down his guard around them. With Wendy, he had no defenses. *How in the world did I get into this mess? I'm going to stay away from her—five feet, minimum.*

She opened a cabinet and wrinkled her cute little nose, then she got up on tiptoes and strained to reach for something. A split second later, she was flat-footed and empty-handed.

One glimpse of her face, and all of Ben's noble intentions fled. He reached her side in an instant and curled his hand around her slender arm. "Are you all right?"

"Fine. Okay, maybe a bit frustrated. You keep essential stuff too high for me to reach." She nervously glanced at the living room, then turned big, pleading eyes to him. "Could you please hand me the nutmeg?"

Ben didn't even know he had nutmeg. As he located it among the other tiny bottles and passed it to her, he murmured under his breath, "I don't want you killing yourself."

"You don't need to worry."

He tucked his arm around her, as much to hold her as to halt her almost frantic moves. A delightful pink suffused her cheeks. Though that change reassured him, he still ordered softly, "Ask me to reach for things. We both know you could use a little help. It's crazy to try to stretch this supper so it'll feed three more big men. I have half a mind to toss them all out of here."

Her gaze captured his. "It's okay. Really."

"Are you sure?"

"I'm telling you, Ben," a smile colored her voice and put an impish sparkle in her eyes, "I know what I'm doing."

"It sure is nice," Harry said, "seeing a woman in the kitchen."

Wendy crooked a brow and separated from Ben. "There were more men than women at the culinary institute."

"Glory," Cletus breathed reverently, "you mean you're a real cook?"

Ben wheeled around. He stared in amazement as Wendy tossed spices into a bowl and blithely corrected his friend. "Chef."

"For real?" Harry nearly slobbered.

She laughed breezily. "No kidding. I work at Papier Luné."

Cletus sighed again. "French. Fancy French chow. Imagine!"

Wendy shrugged. "Some French. Our cuisine is international. We cater to exclusive clientele and adapt our fare as the need arises."

Ben wanted to shove all three men out the door. He'd secretly hoped to somehow tempt Wendy to stay or arrange something—heaven only knew what—but that was a pipe dream. She could go back to Los Angeles and continue to work at that pricey restaurant just as soon as she rid herself of Troy. Keeping an ordinary woman here was impossible, and she'd turned out to be extraordinary. She boasted a special skill. A marvelous, mysterious skill—one that took instant food and turned it into a gourmet meal.

Humming under her breath, she mixed, whisked, and banged pots and pans, and in less than fifteen minutes added to what she'd already made and had a meal for three more hungry men. Nothing half as delectable had ever graced his humble table. He didn't have a clue what she'd added to the instant potatoes, but flecks of things sprinkled across the top of them gave off an aroma that left him drooling.

The canned vegetables didn't look gray and smooshy. They were bright and crisp.

As if that weren't already miraculous enough, she'd used the butter, oatmeal, and canned fruit, then added several odds and ends to concoct some kind of cobbler. She'd created and stuck it in the oven as if the task rated as no more difficult than tossing out garbage.

The last time he'd had cobbler was back when Laura's junior high school counselor stuck her in home economics. Her rendition of the dessert tasted so awful, he'd waited until she'd turned her head and dumped it into his napkin. He wondered if she'd ever improved her kitchen skills. Had she been a better mother than a cook?

"Ben?"

"Huh?" Great, Hawthorne, sound real intelligent.

Wendy smiled at him. "Could you please put on some music?"

Harry loped over to the sound system and called out, "Take your pick: Debussy, Old Time Hymns on Appalachian Dulcimer, Jars of Clay, or Celtic Harp."

Ben felt Wendy's questioning gaze and shrugged. "I have eclectic taste."

"A well-rounded man."

Her compliment meant more to him than it probably ought to. He still basked in it and urged, "Choose what you like."

"I like 'em all. Harry, why don't you play the dulcimer hymns first?"

"Wow," Harry mumbled, "a real meal. A real table cloth. Music. What next?"

Gil said quietly, "I like it." He traipsed into the kitchen. "What about Junior's supper? Is he having some of the 'tatoes and gravy?"

"No!" Wendy grabbed the spoon from his hand to keep him from offering Troy a bite. "Sorry. I didn't mean to startle you. He's allergic to beef. I'm not sure about moose."

He twitched her an understanding smile but said nothing.

Ben felt like a heel. Gil's wife had promised to bring their boys up as soon as he built a place. He'd come, stayed with Ben, and put up a cabin. He'd sent her pictures, proudly chronicling the cabin's construction. When he sent for her, she finally broke the news: She and the boys weren't coming. She'd taken up with his best friend. Now Harry and Cletus lived with him and tried to keep him busy, but he'd been terribly depressed. With nothing to go home to, he'd stayed in Alaska and worked extra hours at the pumping station just to keep his mind off of the family he'd lost. Ben had grumbled about Troy, yet Gil desperately longed for his sons. Ben's insensitivity made him sick.

Wendy asked no questions. She set down the large serving spoon and tapped the tops of the two jars of baby food that sat ready on the counter. Nonchalantly, she turned her back, opened a drawer, and took out Troy's bib and baby spoon.

Gil reached over and swiped them from her. "I don't see a high chair. He'll just have to sit on my lap." No one had the nerve to challenge his assertion.

Ben wasn't about to have these men surround Wendy. He shoved the bowl of potatoes into Harry's hands, quickly lifted the meat platter and thrust it at Cletus, and picked up the vegetables with his left hand. His right hand slid around Wendy's waist and guided her to the small table. That proprietary and possessive move wasn't lost on the men. Harry's brows lifted, and Cletus winked. Gil looked away.

Good. I don't want them sniffing around her. I mean here. Oh, who am I kidding? As long as she's here, she's mine.

He set down the vegetables, then pulled out the chair for her. "Thanks, Cookie," he murmured in her ear. "Supper is wonderful."

She flashed him a quicksilver smile.

He fought the urge to brush a kiss on her cheek. Instead, he rested his hands on her shoulders, ran his thumbs up and down the back of her neck in a tiny, soothing massage, and breathed over her shoulder, "Better make this grace short and sweet. These guys haven't eaten this well in ages. You might very well open your eyes and find they've already inhaled every last morsel."

She laughed, cast a glance at the vacant seat next to herself, and folded her hands. "I'll wait for you."

"I forgot to get napkins."

"Oh." Her muscles tensed as she began to rise.

He gently pushed her back down. "I'll get them as soon as you've prayed."

His friends all shoved their hands into their laps and bowed their heads. Wendy offered a short, heartfelt prayer, and everyone chimed in with a robust "amen!"

Ben patted her shoulder. "Go ahead and serve yourself some of the meat. If Cletus gets it first, you'll end up starving."

Cletus looked at the mooseloaf, then at Harry. "Ben's one to speak. He didn't grow to that size by dieting on celery."

Ben tossed napkins at his friends, sat next to Wendy, and winked. He really wanted to stroke her, twine his fingers with hers. . . . Maybe it was a good thing the guys had dropped by. He'd probably have made a fool of himself if he'd been alone with her.

Harry dumped a mountain of mashed potatoes on his plate. "Gil's the surprising one. He can eat both of us under the table. I don't know where he stuffs it all."

Gil chuckled. He'd been spooning food into Troy quite steadily. "This little guy packs it in too."

"He has a monster appetite," Wendy agreed.

Her voice softened, just as her expression did each time she looked at, touched, or spoke of the baby. Ben stopped ladling gravy onto his food and looked at her. Wife and mother material—unadulterated, genuine, undiluted, and undeniable. He let out a silent sigh. But she's a city girl and can hardly wait to get back to a kitchen at some fancy five-star restaurant. Forget it— she'd never be content in Caribou Crossing.

He started talking about work. Wendy asked a few intelligent questions, but for the most part, she let the men carry the conversation. She ate modestly; he and the men demolished every last bite.

Ding. She blotted her mouth. "Excuse me." She rose and answered the oven timer's call.

Ben sprang to his feet. "Wait!"

She gave him a quizzical look.

"I'll get that. You've already done more than enough work." He plucked the hotpads from her hands and used his thigh to gently nudge her hip. She shuffled to the side. As soon as he opened the oven door, the heavenly fragrance of mingled fruits and spices wafted out and filled the cabin. "You guys had better clear off the table, or I'll shove you all out the door so Wendy and I can eat this alone."

"Not a chance!" Harry bolted to his feet. "Cletus, grab the

plates. Gil—oh, never you mind. Ma'am, we'll do the dishes. You just go sit down and guard that dessert so Ben doesn't gobble it all up."

She laughed. "It needs to cool a bit."

"Whew!" Cletus set an armful of dishes into the sink.

"Whew is right," Wendy said. She sat down and grinned at Ben. Her eyes danced with mirth. "Um, Ben? Troy, uh, needs some. . .attention."

Gil held him out. "Yep. He's ripe. I'll pass him on to you."

Ben glared at them all. "Thanks a heap."

Half an hour later, they'd decimated the cobbler. Harry patted his belly. "Guess I ought to come clean. It isn't poker night. We don't even play poker."

Wendy feigned astonishment. "Really?"

"Makes me feel right sorry for lying," Cletus confessed. "You fed us so nice."

"The good company made up for the bad ruse," she said graciously.

Ben felt proud of her. She'd been a good sport. Not many women would appreciate such a shenanigan, and they'd probably endure it only by dint of marriage. Wendy was his guest, yet she'd shown true Klondike hospitality. He watched as she slipped from the room. A moment later, he sensed her return before he even saw her. He was electrically aware of her presence. Though he considered the cabin comfortable, she'd pulled on a sweatshirt.

Only a few feet into the room, she stopped. Harry had gone over to intercept her. Harry tamed his normally loud voice into a soft whisper, so Ben couldn't hear a word he said. Whatever he murmured, Wendy didn't care for it one bit. Her eyes grew enormous, and the color drained from her face. She wrapped her arms around her ribs and inched back as she shook her head. Ben bolted to his feet and paced over to run interference. His blood boiled.

"Think about it," Harry said.

Ben stormed past his uninvited guest and planted himself

directly beside Wendy. He glowered.

Harry backed off and grabbed his coat. "Guess we'll be going now."

"'Less you wanna go on ahead and play cards," Cletus tacked on in a hopeful tone.

"Get out of here—all of you." Ben tossed Gil and Cletus their coats. His voice was supposed to sound jovial, but it still held a distinct proprietary and warning edge.

Once they were gone, he turned back to Wendy. His eyes narrowed as he studied her intently. She'd been fine until the last few minutes, but something had gone wrong. Terribly wrong. Eyes huge and dilated, she stared back at him, watchful and wary.

He started to reach for her. "Wendy—"

She blinked and changed right in front of his eyes. Her shoulders straightened, and she cut in before he could ask any questions. "Troy's starting to wind up. Gil fed him, but you'd better grab a bottle."

Sidetracked, Ben gave Troy a bottle to hold, then awkwardly tried to balance the little guy and simultaneously sponge off the table. "Two hands aren't enough when you have a kid around."

"Tell me about it. I'll admit, you can't manage entirely on your own. You'll need some breathing space, so I'd suggest finding someone who can watch him here and there as well as when you're at work." She bumped him out of the way and took over the sponge. "My brother lent a hand in the evenings after he got home. It helped tremendously."

"You've mentioned your brother a couple of times. What about parents?"

"They died in a boating accident a few years ago."

"I'm sorry." He brushed a few soap bubbles from her hand in a comforting manner. "So your brother lives with you?"

"No, I live with him."

"That's an unusual arrangement, isn't it?"

Her expression went hard. "I had reasons."

Clearly, he'd stomped on her feelings with that ill-advised comment so he changed the topic. "Speaking of family, I was thinking that Laura might have changed. I only remember her as being a scatterbrained preadolescent. She did ditzy things like getting a loud pink nail polish on the living room carpeting because she didn't let her toenails dry. Another time, she used laundry detergent in the dishwasher because we ran out of the right stuff. It bubbled out and covered the entire floor."

"Your parents must have had a fit!"

He shrugged. "They fought too much to pay any attention. The marriage was doomed from the start. I couldn't believe they kept it patched together for almost four years."

"Maybe Laura wasn't scatterbrained as much as seeking attention."

"You may have a valid point." Ben sat back down at the table. It felt safer given that Troy wiggled like a salmon going upstream. "They virtually ignored us. I was old enough to take things in stride. Laura got short shrift. Still, the thought of her trying to manage Troy is laughable."

Wendy sat at the table, shoved a mug of coffee at him, and took a sip out of her own. He nodded at his mug. "I admit, I really wondered about your sanity when you put eggshells in the coffee grounds. But whatever made you do it, they really improved the flavor—made it mellow."

She shrugged. After a pause, she took another sip and said, "Not to speak ill of your sister, but she didn't have the personality of an ultra-organized individual. Mike teased her by saying if they hired a nanny, she'd be busier watching after Laura than taking care of Troy.

"There's a job that would drive me nuts. Can you imagine watching someone else's kids?"

Giving him a long, meaningful stare, Wendy finally raised her brows.

He had the grace to flush. "That was pretty dumb, wasn't it? You've spent the last four weeks doing just that."

"Five weeks as of today."

Propping his elbows on the table, he beamed at her. "Tell me you've fallen madly in love with Troy and want him to be yours." A flood of emotions broke across her features, but before she could say a word, he pressed on. "Hey, don't get peeved at me for calling things like I see them. Troy and you make a great team."

"You didn't take any mind-altering substances before you came home from work, did you? Because that's the only explanation for you holding such delusional thoughts."

"You're the one with delusional thinking—you hauled Troy up here, assuming I wanted him."

Wendy pushed her mug away. "I assumed nothing of the sort. You agreed to take him. You assumed it was that log cabin company on the radio, and now you're mad at me because you messed up."

"I'm not going to get caught up in that kind of blame game. Plain and simple, the only way he's staying in Alaska is if you move up here and adopt him. You can live with me—"

"Stop right there." She leaped up from the table.

"Where do you think you're going?" He held her shoulder in one huge hand and turned her around to face him once again. Troy was slumped in half over his other arm like a sack of potatoes.

"I'm getting my things. I'm leaving. Now."

He looked at her with complete astonishment. "You're serious!"

"I'm not about to stick around here for even one more day and foster the ridiculous notion that I'm willing to shack up with someone."

"Wendy, grow up. I didn't ask for anything immoral at all. You and Troy are welcome to stay here until I can get another cabin built for you. I simply made the offer, but I wasn't asking anything of you at all."

Her hair swished across her shoulders as she violently

shook her head. "You're trying to saddle me with Troy. Don't act like you're some kind of choir boy."

He let out a rusty chuckle. "You've never heard me sing—with a voice like mine, they'd beg me not to join a choir."

She groaned. "Stop trying to be funny, Ben. Humor isn't working for me—not with this."

"Okay. You want total honesty, then here you go: You're a beautiful woman, and I'm almost a hermit. You turned up and flipped my world upside down. I don't even remember the last time I saw a woman who wasn't Athabaskan other than Janet, and she's seven months pregnant."

"I'm sure those women are delighted that you find them so unattractive," she snapped.

"I didn't say that they were ugly, Wendy. Men fall all over themselves for the women up here. Look at what my friends just pulled simply to be around a woman!"

Wendy knew he was more than right with that observation. Harry had shocked the socks off of her, asking if he could start writing her in hopes she'd become his mail-order bride. Her friends teased her about coming up here to snag a man, but that was the farthest thing from her mind. After a year, she'd barely come to grips with her broken engagement—the last thing she wanted was to leap back into dating, let alone marriage.

Ignorant of her thoughts, Ben kept speaking. "As for the Athabaskan women, their men are extremely protective and possessive. I just meant that some of them are already taken and I'm not particularly attracted by the ones who are unattached. I happen to have a preference for lighter hair," he paused and looked at her intently as his voice took on a deeper timbre, "and green eyes."

"I'm not interested in hearing this." She locked eyes with him. "I'm not here on some crazy find-a-new-life scheme. I only came to find Troy a good home."

"You're not going to find it here."

"You promised to try."

Troy let out a squawk, so Ben rearranged him, then glowered at her. "I liked things much better when I thought you'd come to be my housekeeper."

"It seems as if you had additional duties you expected of that woman."

"I didn't expect anything lurid. I did hope," he confessed in a soft, almost plaintive tone, "maybe since I've had time to mature spiritually, I could enjoy a wholesome relationship with a woman. It's lonely here. Companionship—out of the bedroom—would be welcome."

"I'm not interested, and I'm not sticking around."

He juggled to keep hold of Troy. "Wendy, cool off and let's bathe the kid. You're not thinking straight. If you were, you'd realize I'm no threat."

"Pardon me for not buying that line. I made that mistake once before, and it nearly destroyed me." As soon as the words were out, she regretted having said a thing. She compressed her lips and cranked her head to the side.

A tense silence stretched between them. Ben finally twisted Troy around and chuckled as Troy babbled a singsong stream of syllables. "I guess I'd better gather together all of the necessary gear for bath time, huh?"

"I told you, you had it in you to take care of him. You're learning."

He muttered under his breath as he walked away, "I'd rather learn how to fry eggs."

"Oh, go get some towels."

"Okay, okay." He asked Troy, "Is she always this bossy? I thought that after having a few nights of sleep, she'd mellow out."

"I haven't gotten any sleep!"

"Sure, you have."

Her glare practically singed him. "No, I haven't. You stuck him in bed with me the first night."

"Okay, Wendy, I grant you that, but last night, he—"

"Last night, you didn't get up with him even once."

"He slept."

"Oh, no, he didn't."

"He didn't?" Ben echoed. His face turned into a picture of absolute astonishment.

"No, he didn't."

"Then that cinches it. I can't keep him. I don't even wake up when he cries."

"You wouldn't even wake up when I jostled you."

"You were in my bedroom?" When she nodded, he decided, "You're exaggerating. You must have just stood in the doorway."

"Guess again, Ben. I tucked Troy in next to you. All you did was snore."

Disgruntled at how gratingly cheerful she acted at having sneaked in and listened to him snore, he groused, "Aren't you supposed to be showing me how to give him a bath?"

Wendy insisted that he bathe the baby as she talked him through the process. Troy sat in the sink, screeched delightedly, and splashed like the duck. Ben quickly learned to put the soap out of reach because the boy wanted to eat it. "Probably tastes better than those baby hot dogs," he muttered.

"You might want to think about pinning a towel to your front the next time," Wendy advised. "That's what Bruce did. You're getting soaked."

"I don't mind being wet." Ben tickled Troy's belly and chuckled. "Is he always this playful?"

"Yes, you are, you little dumpling."

"Are you calling me Dumpling?" He lifted Troy from the sink.

"Him, not you, you lug."

"I'm wounded."

Wendy chortled as Troy soaked the front of Ben's shirt. "I don't know about wounded, but you're definitely all wet."

"Arghh!"

"I thought you didn't mind getting wet."

six

With Troy full and bathed, they put him to bed in the playpen. Ben bargained, "If you let me shower first, I'll clean up the place."

"You'll clean up the house, regardless. I did my fair share by cooking supper—more than my fair share."

"I know, but—" He glanced down at his soaked shirt and gave her a pleading, puppy dog look. "Have a heart, Wendy."

"Okay, but only if you take a quick one."

"I'm bigger. It takes me more time because there's more of me."

"That has to be the lamest excuse I've ever heard." She rested her hands on her hips and gave him an exasperated look.

Ben sidled up and took her hands off her hips. He held them and let his gaze roam over her momentarily. The fact that he liked what he saw was clearly reflected in his eyes.

"All right. I'm wrong. It should take you far longer than it takes me." He strategically waited a heartbeat before adding on, "Women seem to like to pamper and pretty themselves. You go first. Take all the time you want—but believe me, you don't need to do a thing to look great."

Wendy yanked her hands from his.

Ben tilted his head to the side and scanned her form more critically. Heat flooded her cheeks in those brief moments. His eyes met hers again. "If the fact that I was merely looking at you makes you blush, then commenting on what I see ought to send you into hysterics."

"I'm here to drop off Troy. I have a job and friends—a whole life waiting back in civilization. Don't confuse the issues or try to play games with me." She wheeled around and disappeared into the bathroom. Seeing him wince at that proclamation hadn't given her any satisfaction whatsoever.

The living room was straightened up and the kitchen counters gleamed when she emerged. Ben had taken off the wet shirt and fidgeted with the vacuum, but he hadn't turned it on. She nodded at it. "He'll sleep through that."

"Are you kidding?"

"Nope. Droning sounds don't faze kids. Loud or sudden noises wake them up."

"Then he'll wake up for sure. Some vacuums might be quiet, but this one sounds like an antique biplane."

"I don't want to argue."

"Go to bed, Wendy." He shot her a smile that made it clear he was going to say something completely outrageous. "You've become absolutely impossible, and I thought maybe a shower would help. To my dismay, it obviously didn't. You were supposed to scrub the prickles off of those delicious curves, but I can see you must not have done a thorough job."

"Can you just give this a break? You tease worse than my brother."

He gave her a purely masculine grin that made him look like an irrepressible rascal. The appearance wasn't deceiving either. Once he'd decided to be a scamp, he didn't stop. "You're not being fair. Even when you bristle, you're enticing."

"Believe me, I'm not interested in enticing any man."

"Too late." He waggled his brows.

She didn't return the smile. "You aren't interested in being tied down with a family, Ben, and I want nothing to do with you or any other man."

"You did okay with the guys tonight."

"Groups are tolerable. One-on-one isn't," she said in a strained tone.

Slowly brushing back a few of her curls, he sympathetically asked, "He really hurt you, didn't he?"

"Yes," she clipped as memories welled up.

"Come here." His growl half invited, half demanded her

presence. He didn't wait for her to comply, but merely scooped her up and carried her to the sofa.

Wendy spluttered helplessly, unsure of how to interpret his actions. His impulsive action startled her.

He sat sideways on the couch, with his back against the arm, and turned her so her spine rested against him. Seated as they were, he curled around the entire length of her back and engulfed her with one arm. His other hand came up and petted her hair as he murmured against her cheek, "You're safe here."

His actions and words were so unexpected, she found it hard to catch her breath. A shiver tingled through her.

"Are you cold?"

"I–I'm fine." She tried to draw away.

"From the first minute I saw you, I've wanted to gather you up and hold you. I secretly wondered why a woman like you would come to Alaska, and I thought maybe you were running from something painful. It isn't often I feel protective. You struck that chord, but I let the baby sidetrack me."

Craning her head so she could look at him better, she denied, "I'm not running, Ben. I just came to deliver Troy."

He petted her hair and shook his head. "Maybe you did come to give me Troy, but you're still nursing a broken heart."

Letting out a choppy breath, she turned away.

"It may not be any of my business, but how did you get engaged to a creep?" He stroked her arm gently. She remained completely silent, and he urged softly, "Tell me all about it so we clear the air. Human nature being what it is, I'll wonder what happened."

"It's not important. I'll be leaving in just a few days."

She let out a choppy sigh. Not that he'd badger her—she sensed he'd actually let her go—but he'd give her wondering glances, and that would drive her nuts after just a few minutes. It was probably best if she gave him a thumbnail sketch so he'd leave her alone.

"I was a fool."

He gently feathered a few errant curls behind her ear. "How?"

"Larry came to a singles' night at church. I just assumed he was a believer. After a few dates, I realized he wasn't a Christian, but I figured if we did church functions as our dates, he'd turn his heart to the Lord." She hung her head and mumbled, "I was wrong. I knew better than to be unequally yoked, yet I deluded myself. I put my own heart on the line."

"And he crushed your heart." He murmured the words compassionately.

"Two months before the wedding, he dumped me. I'd gone to the doctor, and because of some problems I had, the doctor did tests. He warned us my chances of conceiving were small." She paused, then added, "I got burned because I didn't keep God first in my heart. Dumbest thing I ever did."

Ben turned her to the side so she had to face him. He studied her intently for a long stretch of time. "Letting go of you was the dumbest thing that guy ever did. At the risk of being insensitive, I think you're lucky he bailed out. A man who treats his woman like that would make a lousy husband."

"A woman who ignores her soul to follow her heart doesn't deserve—"

"Whoa," he interrupted her. "You've recommitted your heart. Stop punishing yourself." He slowly rubbed his thumb across the galloping pulse at her wrist. "I'm impressed by how you've forged past a rough time and put your life back together."

"I'm not all that 'together' yet. I'm still keeping God busy."

His hand curled around hers, enveloping it in strength and warmth. Ben looked deep into her eyes. "God's done far better than you allow yourself to believe. If I could give you the gift of confidence, I would. I'll pray for you because I know the Lord can heal your heart completely."

His words soothed her. Between the canceled wedding and tuition loans, she'd been too poor to live on her own. Her brother had taken her in, and close friends knew she was struggling to patch together her life. She felt emotionally raw, but Ben's tender acceptance meant the world to her.

She sighed, then confessed, "It's no secret, Ben. I love little Troy. If I were to follow my heart, I'd take him in a flash, but I already made a devastating mistake—following my heart when my head and soul told me not to. I learned my lesson."

"This is different."

She shook her head sadly. "No, it isn't. As much as I want Troy as my own, God hasn't given me peace about keeping him. Believe me, I've prayed and begged."

"Don't you think maybe the fact that I've suggested it and can help you out financially are His way of giving you a go-ahead?"

Tears welled up. "Oh, Ben, I wish that were the case. I've tried to tell myself that, but each time I pray, I come away with the overwhelming sense that Troy is supposed to stay here."

They sat in silence. Finally, Ben gave her a squeeze and asked, "How quick are you with puzzles?"

"Puzzles? I haven't done one in years. Why?"

"Then we'll do one at the dining table. If you were a whiz, we'd use the coffee table, but you'll need it to change Squirt's shorts during the daytime."

Grateful he'd found a way to change the subject, Wendy went to the trestle table. Soon, they were fitting together tiny pieces. Wendy consulted the picture on the box. "Flowers, left bottom corner. You know, this is a beautiful scene."

"It's my backyard."

She gave him a surprised look.

"I took the photo from the back door late in the spring. There's a company that makes puzzles from snapshots. The whole field was covered in forget-me-nots, Alaska's state flower."

"Okay, so I'm not sure what to be more impressed about— your skill with a camera, your scenery, or the fact that you can identify a flower that's something other than a rose or a carnation."

Ben grinned. "I love Caribou Crossing. When I first arrived, I got some books on the flora and fauna. No fair reading them until you finish the puzzle, though."

Wendy tried unsuccessfully to snap a piece into place. "I won't be here that long."

"You're just turned around a bit." He curled two fingers around hers and gave the piece a quarter twist. It snapped into place perfectly. He smiled, then said quietly, "Sometimes, you just need a nudge to find the right fit."

Troy started to whimper.

Wendy automatically tried to get up, but Ben pushed her back down. "Stay here. I'll check on him."

"Honestly, it's time for me to get ready for bed, anyway. I'll see to him, and you can take the next turn by getting up with him during the night."

"You left the door shut, and the thermostat drops during the day. Since it's my spare room, I sealed the vent to cut down on heating costs. The room is too chilly when you leave the door closed all day. I'll open the vent, but it's like closing the gate after the horse bolted. Why don't we trade beds tonight?"

She shifted. "I'll just lie on the couch."

Troy's noise escalated quickly.

Ben got up. "I'd better get him before he sets off an avalanche." He placed Troy on the coffee table and proceeded to change his diaper. "Don't you dare tell anyone I'm actually competent at this. I'd never live it down!"

"Ahem. The guys already found out."

Ben shot her a dark look, and she shrugged.

"Okay. I won't tell anyone else. Mum's the word." Wendy sat up and watched him finish snapping up the fuzzy blue blanket sleeper.

"No, I think that 'hungry' is the word." Ben chuckled and lifted Troy, who was almost frantic. When Wendy reached for the baby, Ben shook his head. "Cuddle up on the couch, Cookie. You're tired, and he's obviously hungry." When she opened her mouth to protest, he gave her a stern look.

"And you told Troy I'm bossy?" Wendy sank onto the cushions.

"Shush and go to sleep. I'll feed him since he's about to stage a revolt."

"I'll see to him. Go take your shower." Wendy practically snatched Troy and waited until Ben got a bottle from the kitchen. Troy needed a few minutes to settle down and start to suck, then he made a satisfied snort and went half limp with bliss. She snuggled him closer. "There you are, Angel."

The shower was running, so Ben's voice astonished her when it seeped across the room, "There you are, Angel. I think you needed him every bit as much as he needed you."

"I thought you got in the shower."

A big, soft blanket descended on her. A second later, he knelt at the side of the sofa. He rubbed her shoulder for a second and coaxed, "Why don't I put you in my bed tonight, and I'll sleep out here? Troy is so much happier when you cuddle him."

She made a wordless sound of protest.

"Okay, Cookie." He tucked the blanket around them more closely, and she felt herself coasting off to sleep.

Awhile later, Troy whimpered. "Here," a faraway voice bade as big hands gently removed the baby.

She fumbled with the blanket and sleepily murmured, "Sorry. Was he crying too much?"

"Shh," was the only reply. He deftly stole Troy away, then came back. "Sweetie, your room is too cold. Use my bed tonight."

She barely opened her eyes. "I'm fine. Go t' bed."

He sighed, and Wendy heard him grumble, "You're making things too hard for yourself."

❧

Early the next morning, Wendy bolted upright a few seconds after Ben entered the living room. She looked completely flustered.

"Sweetie, go back to sleep. You don't need to get up. It's way too early. The baby is still fast asleep. In fact, why don't you go curl up in my bed?"

"No way."

"Your room is warm, but the bed will be cold."

She stood there and gave him a mutinous look. "I think you'd better find someplace else for me to stay."

He pulled a flannel shirt on over his T-shirt and started to button it without bothering to look down. "No, you're staying here."

"I don't want to. I need to get home, and if I can't, at the very least, I need to live elsewhere and come over during the daytime."

He sat on a chair and pulled on socks. "Wendy, no one up here keeps spare rooms. The cost of heating them is absurdly high. I usually keep my neighbors' guests if there's a need."

"Someone has to have a spare room!"

She'd crossed her arms in front of herself, and she looked to be on the verge of tears.

Ben lumbered over to her and calmly folded her in a bear hug. Forking his hand through her curls, he cupped her head to his chest. "Don't even think about running away. I can't try to give Troy my best effort if you're not here to show me what to do. You know how clueless I am. Staying here isn't just a matter of me having the only vacant room in town; it's an act of mercy on your part."

Her arms wound around his waist. She didn't seem to be conscious of the action, and he didn't dare call her attention to it. Pressing her cheek deeper into his flannel shirt, she said in a thick tone, "I shouldn't stay here."

"This is where you belong. I'll keep you safe and warm, and I think we're doing pretty good with the baby."

"I'm so off balance up here."

He held her and continued to comb his fingers through her hair until she settled down. Tipping her face upward, he tenderly smiled at her. "Wendy, you have it all wrong. If anything,

I'm the one who's off balance."

"Because I'll leave Troy with you?"

"No. Because I'm afraid you just might take my heart away when you leave." He brushed a light kiss on her cheek, then let out a cross between a groan and a sigh. After sweeping her up, he laid her on the couch.

"We both have some learning and growing to do. You're going to stop beating yourself up about the past."

"What are you learning?"

"To my amazement, I'm learning that a baby between us makes no difference."

"Your baby," she whispered in a raw tone. Her hand came up, and she brushed her fingers across her cheek. "You shouldn't have kissed me."

"I've wanted to kiss you ever since I laid eyes on you."

"You don't always get what you want," she muttered.

"This time I do." He knelt beside her and leaned forward. His strong fingers slipped to her nape and kneaded the tension from her neck.

Her hands clutched his wrists. "You'd better go. You'll be late for work."

"I'd like to stay home with you and Troy."

"No."

"I figured you would say that. You're the woman who just informed me I wouldn't always get what I wanted."

She gave him a weak smile.

"I may not have to learn as much about Troy as I have to learn about myself. It's probably a good thing I'm going to work today. I have some serious thinking to do."

She struggled to get up, but he pressed her back down.

"Ben, I was going to make you a lunch."

"Sleep. I'll throw together a few sandwiches." He winked. "Take care of yourself today, Cookie."

seven

A decent night's sleep made a huge difference in her ability to cope. Wendy played with Troy and did a load of laundry. She decided to make Beef Stroganoff for dinner and actually fit in a few minutes here and there to read a magazine article.

Ben got home from work, took one look at her, and broke into a toothy smile. "You look like a new woman!"

"You're the one who accused me of being grumpy because I didn't get enough sleep."

"I was, wasn't I? I was right too!" He peeled off his parka and boots. "What did you and Troy do today?"

"We entertained. A guy named Chuck dropped off his wife. Janet and I visited for awhile—even did a big chunk of the puzzle. She went wild over Troy and said she needs practice with a baby. She said she's due in eight weeks, but from the way she looks, I think she'd better take a crash course."

Ben nodded. "Chuck works with me. I'm not sure who's more antsy—him or her." He gestured toward the floor where Troy lay on a blanket. "Why do you put him down here?"

"He sleeps in the playpen, and I put him there if I need him contained, but it's only fair to let him free so he can wriggle and turn when I'm right on hand."

"Fair enough. Just make sure you put him on a blanket so I can tell where he is. I'm afraid I'll step on the poor tyke and squash him."

"Impossible—he's too noisy. Listen to him."

He tilted his head for a second, then declared, "You talk more than Troy. Isn't that completely predictable."

"I don't know. It seems that a certain male is saying more than enough around here."

"Maybe you're still grumpy, after all." Ignoring her splutter

91

of outrage, he lay down on his belly and peered at Troy. "Hi, Bright Eyes."

Troy squealed and fell from his precarious stance on his hands and knees onto the floor. His happy sounds ended abruptly, and a wail filled the room.

"Ouch! That looked like it hurt."

"So pick him up." Wendy nudged Ben's foot with her toe.

He rolled onto his back and laid Troy on his chest. "Stop whining, Buster. I don't like crybabies." A second later, he made a disgusted sound. "He's sliming me! He's drooling all over. Wendy—"

Laughing as she dropped a burp cloth on him, she warned, "He does that a lot. I think he's trying to get another tooth."

"He's got four. What's the score?"

"Four to nothing?" she ventured, tongue in cheek.

"Don't give up your day job to go into comedy."

She squatted down to wipe Troy's face. Ben tugged on her waist to rob her of her balance, causing her fall flat. The suddenness of the action made her let out a shriek.

Ben chuckled. "Now who's making all of the noise?"

Wendy scooted a bit closer and gently rubbed Troy's hair to tame it down a bit.

Ben cuddled both her and the baby and asked quietly, "I've tried to figure something out. Last night, you said something about not being able to have kids. . . ." His voice trailed off.

She closed her eyes and took a deep breath. "I've always had some problems, but they didn't seem any worse than stuff my friends moaned and complained about. I went to see the doctor two months before I was supposed to get married. He did some tests and told me my chances of conceiving are slim. In a twisted way, I guess maybe it was a blessing. Getting married and having a baby with Larry would have been a disaster."

Ben kissed her forehead and softly nuzzled her temple. "Wendy, I don't understand something. Why did you bring Troy to me when you want a baby so badly yourself?"

Wendy sighed. "I admit, it's the hardest thing I've ever done. I didn't have a choice. Still, it's the right thing to do. You're his family. It's not a matter of what I want. Even if you ignore Laura's wishes and try to arrange things so I can take him, I'll have to refuse."

She traced the tiny cowlick at the back of Troy's head over and over. She knew it by heart—the silky texture and just how the hair went clockwise. This must have been how Abraham felt when he put Isaac on the altar. . . .

She sucked in a choppy breath. "Letting go of Troy will break my heart, Ben. Truly, it will. . .but I have to. I've told you, I have to put my trust in God, and He hasn't given me the assurance that I'm to keep the baby."

He slowly stroked her shoulder and stayed silent for awhile. She stayed silent too. Troy babbled contentedly. Giving him a pat, Ben broke the subdued lull between them, "Hasn't it occurred to you that I'm not really Troy's family either?"

"That isn't the issue. Laura thought of you as family—so much so, she and her husband chose you. You, Ben."

He interrupted. "Did she know about the odds that you'd probably never conceive?"

Wendy shrugged. "I wasn't specific. She knew I wanted a baby, but she also knew I'm alone."

"This is outlandish." Ben shook his head. "It's been twelve years since I saw her. We did the Christmas card thing for a few years, but I moved and lost her address. She must have been living in a fantasy world to imagine me married with a bunch of kids. Why wouldn't she choose someone she saw and knew well?"

"Blood's thicker than water."

"Wendy, Troy and I aren't blood kin. Her whole rationale falls apart."

Flushed and rattled, Wendy blurted out, "Don't expect me to explain—I can't. All I know is, Troy is yours. Don't try to weasel out of it or find excuses. You were chosen and it's only right for you to have him. So stop it." Her voice cracked. "Just stop it!"

&

She'd come completely unglued. Ben knew she was emotionally raw and he'd pushed too many buttons in the last twenty-four hours. He decided to head for neutral ground. He nodded, then tucked her head back on his shoulder and quietly changed the topic. "So tell me about being a chef."

"I went to a culinary institute. I love to cook, so it seemed like a good plan. I landed a job at a four-star restaurant, but because I'm one of the newest chefs, I'm scheduled last and fill in for weird shifts."

"You must have been first in your class. I've never tasted better food."

"Thank you."

"How old are you, Cookie?"

She lifted her head to look at him.

"So I'm being rude. I never have understood why a woman's age is supposed to be a deep, dark secret. I'm thirty-one. You're younger than I, so seniority gives me rank. Answer the question."

She sighed. "I'm twenty-four."

"Is that a mere baby, or is that all grown up?"

"I don't know." She gave him a sweet smile. "Is thirty-one middle aged, or is it decrepit?"

"Stop batting your eyes, you minx." He slid Troy off of his chest, rolled over, and tickled her ribs.

Wriggling, she tried to avoid him but didn't have the ability to get far since she still couldn't move easily. Glorious peals of laughter burst out of her, laced with pleas for mercy. After the way he'd nearly had her in tears moments before, Ben delighted in finding a way to lift her mood.

"Say 'uncle.' "

Her head tipped back, and she let out a trill before breathlessly asserting, "Troy's supposed to call you that."

Letting out a low growl, he nuzzled her neck. "I'm starving."

Grateful that he was still feeling playful, she shoved at him. "Don't be a cannibal."

"Spoilsport! Where's my mooseloaf sandwich, anyway?"

"Your friends ate every last bite of the mooseloaf, and you know it."

"What do I smell, then?"

She rolled onto her side and laughed uproariously. "We have a baby, and you ask me what you're smelling? You're not decrepit, you're insane."

As they finished dinner, Ben mentioned, "This may not exactly be supper conversation, but it's pretty important: I just used the last diaper out of the second bag. Are we going to run out before Saturday?"

Grimacing, she admitted, "I don't know. I hope not. Can't we get diapers from anyone?"

"I don't know. I'll get on the radio and see what I can rustle up."

"Good idea. When will the phone work again?"

"Probably tomorrow."

Wendy wrinkled her nose. "I don't know how you live this way—so out of touch with everyone."

"Think about it: I'm not out of touch at all. I see the guys at work, and folks have made a point to check on you and Troy each day—without me asking them to, I might add. In the big city, you probably don't know more than a few of your neighbors. Here, we all know and help each other. You have this image of being self-reliant, but here, we all know the truth: We survive because we rely on God and one another."

❧

The next morning, Ben flipped eggs and grumbled, "I wrecked them again. I don't care what you say, I'm not cut out to be a cook. I did exactly what you said."

"C'mon, Ben, they'll still taste fine."

"Wanna make a bet?" He pivoted and tilted the pan to show her the charred, gooey mess. "If this were Old Testament times, a priest would categorize it as a burnt offering."

She let out breezy laugh and started to feed Troy. "Your uncle is one of those grumpy, old, I-told-you-so guys. Don't you dare grow up to be like that." A second later, she hopped up. "Wait just a minute. Troy is your responsibility today. You get over here and feed him."

He scraped the egg mess into the trash. "I have something more important to do."

"Oh?"

"I'm taking a snowmobile to the Perns'. They have some cloth diapers they'll loan us."

"Make sure you put Troy in his bunting, then."

He plunged the pan into the sink and scowled at her as if she'd taken leave of her senses. Hooking a thumb into the pocket of his jeans, he asked, "Are you nuts? It's cold out there."

"I know that. I also know other people have reared children in this environment, and those kids were taken out now and again. You have to learn to pack a diaper bag and bundle him along."

"I don't have two snowmobiles, Wendy. You can't come, and I'm not ready to take him anywhere all on my own."

"Nonsense. You can take him in the backpack on the snow-mobile. I'll talk you through the steps of packing the diaper bag, and Mrs. What's-her-name who's giving us the diapers will help you if you hit any snags on her end of the line."

"I'm not interested."

"I don't care whether you're enchanted or repulsed. You have to learn to take him places with you."

"Wendy, don't rattle me."

"Ben, cope."

"I am coping—I'm getting the diapers."

She gritted her teeth and flung back, "The way you're act-ing, you ought to be wearing them yourself!"

He glowered at her and said her name in a low, warning growl. "It'll only take me a little while."

"Good. That'll make your first trip out short and sweet." She plucked the diaper bag from the floor and thrust it at him.

Ben stared at it as if he'd never seen it before. "How can you expect me to know what to stick in here?"

"I'll help you. It's well past time for you to assume the responsibilities and learn the finer points of parenting."

"Fat chance."

Stubbornly crossing her arms across her chest, Wendy snapped, "Fine. Pack it yourself. If you forget anything, a one-hour trip won't be a disaster."

Ben haphazardly shoved in a diaper, grabbed two wipes from the box, and threw them in, soggy and loose. He added a bottle, then zipped the quilted bag shut. "There. I hope you're happy. I did it myself. I'll take him—but when we get back and he's a screaming mess because of the cold, I expect more cooperation and help."

"More cooperation and help?"

He grimly tucked Troy into the backpack carrier and hefted it into place. As he pulled the waist strap tight and stomped to the door, Ben declared, "He's not going to enjoy this."

"Yes, he will. He hasn't been outside since we got here. Neither of us has."

He stopped short and pivoted around. "You haven't taken him out at all?"

"Of course I haven't. I don't own any snow clothes. I can't carry him and keep from slipping and falling, because I don't have skid-proof boots like you do. You've had the freedom to come and go whenever you pleased; I've been cooped up like a criminal."

"Bringing Troy here was a crime!"

Wendy stared at him. "I don't know what your problem is."

"My problem," he gritted, "is that you're trying to be a martyr! You're doing your best to give me a royal guilt trip just because you want Troy for yourself and I don't happen to share your infatuations with babies!"

Ben fought the urge to slam the door behind himself as he made his way to the snowmobile. Troy was still during the whole trip. The sound and motion apparently didn't faze him in the least. To Ben's astonishment, when he pulled Troy from the backpack carrier, the baby wore a huge, toothy smile. Finding the smile irresistible, Ben rubbed noses with the infant and affectionately scolded, "Scamp."

Wila Pern dashed down the stairs. "Give him to me. Where's Wendy?"

"She stayed home."

"Oh, what a pity. I wanted to meet her. I've heard such lovely things about her. Now will you look at this big boy," she cooed as she carried Troy into her cabin.

Ben hadn't had to look farther than Wila for diapers. She was Caribou Crossing's "mother." Anyone who needed help or a shoulder to cry on knew that Wila was always willing and loving. Her husband acted as the lay pastor for the town. Best of all, they never broke a confidence. Wila often cared for her own grandchildren, but any of the families in the area knew they had a standing invitation to use her as a baby-sitter so they could take a little getaway.

"What a delightful baby!"

"He's a big responsibility."

Mark Pern peered at him over the edge of his bifocals. "Ben, your cabin is large and you can have him go to work with you if you need to. Adam's taken his kids in when he needed to. No one objects."

"That's only every once in awhile."

Wila hitched her shoulder as if the matter were of no gravity. "I'll bet Betty Packard or Susan Blossom would be willing to baby-sit. They're both raving about how darling he is."

"I'm not ready to be saddled with a child. Even with daily help, I'm not prepared to keep him. Wila, kids need love."

She shook her gnarled finger at him. "You should love him."

Her husband looked at Ben for a long while, then stated, "That little boy needs a strong man. With God's guidance, you can do it."

"We'll help out," Wila went on. "If you need to go to the city for a few days now and then, we'll keep him for you. God put the boy in your care—He'll give you wisdom and endurance."

She had a bundle ready for him. "Diapers, diaper pins, and plastic pants. Be sure to give them back to me. My little Annie still wears them when she comes to visit."

"Thanks for the loan."

"I put in a baby food grinder too. I didn't know if you had a food processor."

"I don't."

"If you think about it, order one. In the meantime, if you run short of jarred baby food, you can take some of your own food and put it through this mill to grind it up for little Troy."

The idea of pulverizing his food was revolting. "You've got to be kidding me. That sounds nauseating."

"Then do it between your own meals."

Mark frowned at him. "Ben, this isn't like you at all. You're usually even-tempered. I hope the woman who brought him isn't seeing you like this. You're at your worst."

Before he could respond, Wila chimed in. "Howie said she was kind to the baby. Since his plane was fully loaded, she had to hold the baby on her lap all of the way from Fairbanks. She was cold and tired, but she never complained."

"Howie ought to get his head examined for agreeing to bring them here at all."

Wila's dark gaze dealt him a healthy dose of disappointment as she stared at him. She finally said, "Gil says she's gentle and kind. Cletus said she's a great cook."

"Gil's a lonely, hurting man. As for Cletus—feed him, and he'll sing your praises."

Wila's wrinkles scrunched into a displeased array. "It's a good thing folks are dropping by. Wendy must be desperate for someone nice. Susan, Betty, and Janet all spoke well of her. Regardless of what you say about Gil and Cletus, Wendy made a real impression on Harry. Did you know he asked her if they could continue a correspondence because he'd consider her as a mail-order bride?"

"What!"

She nodded sagely. "You've had two diamonds under your roof. You should open your eyes."

"My eyes are wide open. All I see are problems."

"Look harder. God tells us to care for the orphans and widows, and that little boy lost his parents. Instead of focusing on how your life will change, think about how the Lord must have a reason for putting one of His precious orphans in your care. Call one of the women today and make sure she starts coming as soon as Wendy leaves. If you can't cherish him, let him benefit from the love of another until you come to your senses."

"I'm sending him back with Wendy. She knows that's my plan, but she says she needs some kind of heavenly confirmation. Troy belongs with her. I've never been more sure of anything in my life. The truth is staring her in the face, but she's sitting there, waiting for God to paste the kid to her suitcase or something."

Wila shook her head. "Ben, if she's put a fleece before the Lord, that's her business. You're being impatient and unfair. If I had room, I'd invite her to stay with me now. I'm upset by your attitude after ten minutes. She's had five days of it."

His grimace made her cluck in disgust.

"When Saturday comes, she'll be ready to go. How can you ask her to continue to shoulder a burden that you aren't willing to lift yourself?" Wila stuffed Troy back into his bunting. "I think you should go home and spend some time in prayer."

Thoroughly chastened, Ben stuffed the bundle into the nose of his snowmobile and secured Troy on board. The Perns were famed for their hospitality and caring. In the seven years he'd lived in Caribou Crossing, he'd come to know and respect the older couple. He hadn't ever seen them chide or rebuff a soul, yet they'd both made it clear they disapproved of his attitude and disagreed with his decision.

The thought of Harry simply looking at Wendy gave him a pang of jealousy. For Harry to consider marrying Wendy was almost laughable, but Ben's sense of humor wasn't up to entertaining the thought even as a joke. Wendy deserved far better.

He didn't hasten home. Wila's words echoed in his mind, and he needed to consider them. Wendy had forced him to assume some of the responsibilities for Troy's care, and truth be told, he'd actually gotten proficient at doing basic chores for the kid. But Ben admitted to himself that he'd resisted plenty. He squirmed when he recalled their fight before he left. She'd been right too. Troy thoroughly enjoyed the outing, and he hadn't been much trouble.

Ben headed for home. Stepping across the threshold of the back door, he called out Wendy's name, but silence reigned. At first, he thought that maybe she was napping, but that notion died the moment he found the couch and both beds unoccupied. A sense of sick dread welled up. His cabin looked neat and Troy's things still lay about, but Wendy's small suitcase was missing. He dashed to the front door. His heart dropped as he noted a set of prints in the snow.

❧

Wendy didn't see any other choice. Ben continued to rely on her, so he stayed completely blind to the reality of the situation. Troy was his nephew, his responsibility. He needed to try to tend him and determine whether the darling little boychild was really the burden he thought him to be. With her there, he kept depending on her to give the care, to make the decisions, to allow him his freedom without forcing him to assume the obligations.

Calling her a martyr had been the proverbial last straw. This was already a complicated matter, but he'd made it impossible. Admittedly, she'd shocked him by showing up with a baby—still, after almost a week, couldn't he see how sweet Troy was?

Why do I have to give my heart so easily? I got engaged far too fast and got burned. Now, I've lost my heart to Troy. I have to get out of here before I make a fool of myself over Ben. He'll manage with Troy. I'm sure of that much. One minute, he's a terrific guy toward me; the next, he's livid. I can't stay here. Neither of us knows how we feel, but it's clearly a recipe for disaster. I can't stand this heat. Time for me to get out of Ben's kitchen.

At least the dreary gray sky hadn't dumped any more snow today. She ought to be grateful for that. Every day since she'd arrived, flurries had fallen. Wendy used her roiling emotions to fuel her trek. She decided to seek shelter with anyone who would take her in until Saturday rolled around.

She wished she knew where Gil, Harry, and Cletus's cabin was. Surely, they'd take her in. A wry smile twisted her lips. They'd be like Snow White and the three. . .giants? Her life was so warped, she couldn't even get the fairy tale straight. If they wouldn't take her, surely someone in town would oblige. They had to. Staying with Ben had become untenable.

Wendy wore her sweatpants over her jeans and had on both a blouse and a sweatshirt under the light anorak Howie had lent her. She hadn't brought any gloves, so her hands stung. She wore her purse slung over one shoulder and held the suitcase in the opposite hand. When she first set out, she could hardly bear the cold. It sliced right through her clothes. Now, after she'd kept walking, the activity had warmed her to the point she started to perspire. *This is more of a workout than aerobics!*

The way to town wasn't much of a mystery. It lay due west. As it was just morning, Wendy figured she could get there by midafternoon. Oddly enough, she felt a bit drowsy. She promised herself a nice, long nap once she got to shelter. Wendy bowed her head into the wind and tightened her hold on the suitcase, even though she felt her resolve slipping. In the distance, she heard a droning sound. As it got louder, she thought it might be Ben's snowmobile, but she didn't bother to look over her shoulder to confirm her suspicion.

"Wendy!" Ben halted the snowmobile a few yards ahead of her and sprang off. He strode over, stopped dead in front of her, and grabbed her arms. "Are you crazy?"

"Let go of me."

"You're freezing."

"No, I'm not. I'm practically roasting."

His face was thunderous, and his voice shook as he ground out, "You haven't even unzipped—"

Wendy batted his hand away before he could unfasten her zipper. The man had to be crazy if he thought she'd open her anorak out here. "When I get to town—"

"You'll never make it to town. Look at yourself!"

She turned to the side. He caught her arm and steadied her as she almost lost her balance. Angered by his very presence, she gave him a defiant look and clamped her mouth shut.

"Your hands—you're not even wearing gloves. We have to turn back." He yanked the tiny suitcase from her frigid hand and pitched it into the snowmobile. "Come on."

"No."

She took two more steps and managed to slip. The world swirled madly for a split second as she failed to regain her balance and fell flat on her back. She went down so hard, all of the air whooshed out of her lungs. Though momentarily dazed by the jolt, she couldn't catch her breath.

"Wendy!" Ben knelt next to her and sheltered her from the wind. His hands ran over her quickly to be sure she hadn't broken anything. His heart hammered furiously, and he tasted the tang of fear as he strove to reassure them both.

She lay so stunned or hurt, she didn't move at all. *God, let her move. It was a simple slip and fall. Don't let anything be wrong. Don't let it be anything bad.* Ben willed her to move, and an eternity later, she barely shifted. Relief flooded him.

She'd moved her arms ever so slightly, so he allowed himself to lift her head and shoulders out of the snow, cradling her tightly in the crook of his arm. "I have you, Honey. You got the wind knocked out of you. Bend your knees and curl up on your side so you can catch your breath."

Ben realized her pain kept her from following his order, so he nudged her knees close. His gloved hand rested on her cheek for a moment, then slid down to press over hers where it braced the base of her ribs. "Are you okay?"

Her dazed look changed as her eyes brimmed. He suspected

if she opened her mouth, she'd start to cry. As it was, she blinked back the tears at a furious rate.

"Sweetie, talk to me. Are you all right?"

She merely nodded, pushed away, and struggled to her knees. A low, almost breathless moan broke from her lips.

Ben scooped her up. "Come on, Wendy. Put your arms around my neck."

She cringed and turned her face away.

Ben hitched her higher, leaned back to make her tumble against his chest, then squeezed her. He looked down and felt his guts twist as he saw her stricken expression. She'd blanched white as midwinter snow, and her eyes looked haunted. "Honey," he said hoarsely, "I'll make it better. Hold tight."

She still kept one arm across her ribs. The other clenched a fistful of the front of his jacket. She showed more trust and cooperation than he deserved. "That's the way," he praised. "The ride back won't be easy. Hang onto me."

During the precarious and noisy ride, they didn't speak at all. When they reached the cabin, Wendy parted from him at once. She stood out in front of his steps and shook her head as if to refuse to go back inside. Ben took one look at her and knew she'd revolt if given time to marshal her thoughts. He hit her in her most vulnerable spot. "We have to get the baby inside, Wendy. He's been out here too long in this backpack thing. The temperature is dropping, and it's starting to snow again. Come on."

Troy began to wail as if on cue.

Bowing her head in defeat, she trudged up the stairs and went back inside.

Ben got Troy out of his bunting in a flash and stuck him in the playpen. The plastic giraffe waited there, and Troy started to gnaw on him. As soon as his nephew was seen to, Ben turned back to the woman who stood in the entryway, unmoving. "Oh, Sweetie, don't cry," he pled in a soft tone.

His hand came up and brushed tears off of her frigid cheeks. The way she stared at his wet fingers told him she hadn't realized she'd started weeping. Now that he'd made her aware of it, she couldn't stop.

He gathered her close, stood there, and let her cry herself out. How he hated it when a woman cried! He murmured soothing sounds but didn't know what to say. After visiting Wila, he knew that from a woman's perspective, he'd blown it. For Wendy to have walked out on him was completely predictable, though horrifyingly dangerous. Her crying finally tapered off to sniffling hiccups, much to his relief.

Her breaths stayed choppy and uneven, and she shivered in his arms. Whether it was from fear, anger, or cold, he didn't know. He'd deal with her feelings later. For now, he'd minimize the effects of her exposure to the frigid Alaskan weather.

"You're all cold and wet. We have to warm you up right away." Ben stripped off her anorak. He frowned at its thin cloth lining and groaned as he saw the pitiful shirt and sweatshirt she'd layered to keep herself warm. Snow had gotten inside and melted, leaving her soggy and chilled. Worse, though, she'd started to perspire, and that moisture had begun to ice her skin.

"Change into your nightgown. You're suffering from exposure, so we need to put you to bed right away."

Giving him a determined look, Wendy shook her head. "I have to go."

"Come on," he growled. Ben hefted her up and strode toward her bedroom but realized she'd simply shut and lock the door. He quickly diverted back to the sofa. Once there, he set her on her feet and ordered, "Start peeling out of those wet things. I'll get you your nightgown."

Once he stepped away, she didn't move a muscle.

Alarmed that she hadn't followed his directions, Ben grabbed her sweatshirt and hastily tugged it over her head. Bad enough it was soaked, but the wet blouse beneath it clung to her arms and neck, worsening her chill. He yanked her sweatpants down, hoping in vain her jeans would still be dry. Her gasp sounded harsh.

"Hush," he said, his voice rough with concern, but he hoped the way he momentarily stopped and cupped his hands around her waist would make up for his curt word and abrupt actions. She looked at him for an instant, all wide green eyes, before she tried to shimmy away. He held tight. "Wendy, Sweetie, we have to get you out of these wet clothes."

"Leave me alone." She cringed and shivered.

Ben paced over to the entryway, hastily unzipped her suitcase, and returned with her nightgown. "Here, put this on." When she made no move to obey, he shoved the flannel gown at her. "I'll step out of the room and give you two minutes to change. No more than that. You're dangerously cold."

Once he hastened to his bedroom and closed the door, she struggled to change. The dry, long flannel gown looked inviting. Her arms felt heavy as lead, and weariness dragged at her. Peeling off her jeans was so hard, she left them in soggy rings around her ankles. Putting the gown on was a feat.

"Your two minutes are up. Are you decent?"

She gave no response.

Ben's footsteps rang across the floor. He knelt and freed her feet from the jeans and soaking socks.

"Upsy-daisy." He lifted Wendy and put her on the couch. He tossed a blanket over her, and once he plugged the attached cord into the socket, Wendy realized he'd stripped the electric blanket from his own bed. Ben tucked the cover around her shoulders and growled, "I'll be right back. Troy's sounding hungry. He can have a bottle in his playpen."

Wendy closed her eyes and shivered. All she wanted was to go to town. That wasn't asking too much, was it? As soon as she warmed up again, she'd get him to take her. He was so disgusted with her, he'd be glad to wash his hands of them. No, not them, just her. She sobbed.

"Sip." He lifted her head and held something hot to her mouth. She made a halfhearted effort to take a small sip. "Come on, Wendy. Have more." His quiet encouragement wasn't working, so he raised his volume. "Drink this!"

The tea tasted awful. She turned her head, but he demanded so fiercely, she complied just to silence him. As she polished off the last mouthful, she realized he must have dumped half of the sugar bowl into the cup. It tasted dreadful. She wearily rested her head against the back of the sofa.

"Good girl." He pushed her curls away from her face and carefully felt the temperature of her skin.

The next thing she knew, Wendy felt the blankets beside her lift and Ben slide in to nestle close.

Her eyes flew open, and she let out a shrill scream.

Ben captured her and drew her against him. "Body heat transfers best and fastest. You're dangerously cold, Cookie." He sucked in a pained breath and accused, "Your feet are like ice cubes!"

Her teeth chattered as she declared, "I didn't ask you to find out!"

"Sweetie, I let you get into your gown. I need to warm you up, but I thought that would reassure you that I'm not going to take advantage of the situation." His hands kneaded and rubbed her purposefully. "You have on your gown, and I put on these cutoffs so you'd be comfortable with me—"

"I'll warm up on my own." The shiver that tingled down her spine spoiled her assertion. She'd never felt so cold and miserable. The original numbness began to wear off. A million icy needles pricked her, tortured every inch of her flesh. His warm hands soothed away the feeling, but they left an equally disturbing sensation in their wake.

"Good girl." His breath flowed across her neck, and his lips warmed her cold-stung ear. Even with those sensations, she stayed entirely motionless. "Hold still. Just like that. Let me do the work. I'll warm you up."

"Please, Ben," she whispered in a thin, horrified tone.

"Wendy, I want you to listen to me. This is important. This whole thing with Troy has shaken me up, and I ended up taking it out on you. I acted like a total jerk this morning." He squeezed her a bit tighter, and his voice dropped in volume and tone. "Honey, I'm so sorry."

She could scarcely imagine he'd transformed into a decent, caring human being after he'd been so nasty this morning.

He kept hold of her, but he was careful to avoid taking advantage of the situation. His chest rose and fell, pressing him closer to her, warming her. He gently rubbed her arms. "I know your heart is troubled and hurting, and I made it worse by being insensitive."

She shivered.

He moaned, "Oh, Wendy, I hope that's because you need to warm up a little more. We'll work through this."

Several minutes later, he rumbled in a teasing tone, "You're warming up a bit. I'd judge you to be about half baked." He eased his fierce bear hug and waited as she stayed there, unmoving. When he was sure she wasn't just resting a moment, Ben reached over and smoothed his fingers down her cheek and across her jaw. He tenderly turned her face and forced her to look at him. "I know you're tired, but that's a warning sign for hypothermia. We have to finish warming you up. It takes time for your core temperature to come back up. I'll put you down here and go light a fire."

"No."

A small spark of hope lit in his heart. "I'll be right back, Honey. I'll keep holding you."

Her brow puckered, and she made a small, distressed sound he didn't know how to interpret. After taking a few deep breaths, he tested her skin and admitted hoarsely, "I think you're warm enough that the electric blanket will kick in now. I'd better bail out before I forget my good intentions."

She felt flustered, more at herself than at his actions. He'd been sincere with his apology. He'd also been honorable. As a Christian, she'd decided she wanted to follow Christ's instructions to forgive a brother, just as He had forgiven her. Still, the vulnerability she felt scared her.

Ben caressed her cheek gently. "I know you're tired. Cold exposure does that. Taking care of Troy made you tired too.

You can nap for a long time."

She shook her head.

"Sure you can, Sweetie."

"I have to go to town."

Rubbing his forehead against hers, he denied softly, "No, you don't. You're where you belong. Now go to sleep."

She felt hot tears slip down her cheeks. She tried to convince herself as much as she tried to convince him when she trembled, "I don't want to be here. I don't."

"I know." His voice actually sounded pained. He sipped away her tears.

She barely muffled a sob.

"Oh, Wendy," he sighed. He gave her a hug, then inched away a bit. His voice went rough with emotion. "For a moment, let go. Just for now. Let me take care of you. I'll see to the baby all by myself too."

"Tomorrow—" she started to say in a thin voice.

"Don't worry about later. We'll work things out. Be warm. Coast off."

"At least let me go to my room."

"That bed is cold, Wendy. You need this heat."

She couldn't help herself. Overwhelmed, she wailed, "Can't you ever compromise?"

He let out a slow gust of air. "I can see why you feel that way. Come on, then." He gathered her in his arms and carried her into the spare bedroom. Ben held and carried her easily, even kept her sheltered in one arm as he stooped and flung back the covers on her bed. He lowered her onto the cold sheets and grimaced. Ben wiped the tears from her still-cool cheeks and shook his head.

Wendy missed his strength and heat, but she'd never admit it. She bit her lip and tried to curl onto her side. As soon as she started to move, he guided her over. She was shocked at how weak she felt. Had he not helped her, she wouldn't have made it. Once he withdrew his touch, she felt bereft. How could that be when she didn't want or need him?

He slowly drew the covers up and cuffed them at her neck. Compared to the security of his arms when he'd enveloped her, their meager weight made the chill grow worse. His fingers brushed her hair in a momentary caress, then he left without saying another word. A moment later, he spread the electric blanket over her and knelt to plug it in.

Wendy closed her eyes, trying to ignore his presence and struggling to keep from crying. She heard his muffled grunt as he stretched to reach the outlet, then felt his closeness as he stayed at the bedside.

Ben very gently smoothed her hair, then tucked the blankets tightly around her and added a few more. Clearly, he thought she'd fallen asleep. He leaned closer and curled himself around her shoulders in a purely protective, warming move, and she vaguely heard muffled snippets of his prayer as she drifted off to sleep.

Wendy stayed in her room at lunch and refused even to go to the door. In truth, she'd slept quite awhile, but when she awoke and remembered the way he'd cared for her, she felt confused. The last thing she needed was to lose her heart again. Keeping Ben at arm's length was absolutely necessary for her peace of mind.

≈

By supper, Ben heard Wendy rustle around and knew that she had to come out, if only to use the bathroom. He'd taken care of Troy all day, and it was demanding; still, it hadn't been completely impossible.

"Cookie, I'm broiling some salmon fillets for chow. Come on out."

She opened the door and kept her gaze trained at the floor. "Don't call me that."

"Don't call you—oh." He felt an odd stab of disappointment. He liked his sobriquet for her. It had come about so naturally, and she was such a sweet treat in his life that it fit her. For her to reject his special nickname for her felt like she rejected him. He wasn't ready for that either, but he was savvy enough to know arguing with her at this point would yield disastrous results.

"Where is my suitcase?"

"Behind the left chair."

She shuffled over and plucked her robe from the case. Turning her back on him, she put it on and tied the sash tightly. She went back to the bedroom, and he worried that she'd stay there. To his relief, she didn't. She reappeared a second later with a puzzled frown. "My clothes?"

He paused for a moment, then confessed, "I forgot all about them. I'll wash them after supper."

"Don't bother. I can do it." She headed for the soggy pile by the couch.

"The fish is ready. We'll see to that later. I ought to warn you that this is about the only decent thing I can cook. I went fishing with Howie and Gil last the spring and caught quite a few of these beauties.

Placing the plates on the table, Ben commented, "I'm not the most observant man in the world. I hadn't realized you only had two outfits with you. Maybe I have something around here you can borrow."

She put Troy into the playpen. "I'll be okay once I wash those things."

Ben led her to the table and scooted in her seat. He pitched his voice low and still. "I know the Rivians have warm clothes."

"At least something is warm up here."

In the interest of diplomacy, he didn't laugh. They ate in virtual silence. Troy started to fuss, and Ben calmly perched the tyke on his lap and tried to feed him a small bite of shredded salmon. Troy took it and grinned. A dozen bites later, he lost interest, but Ben chuckled, "So he's a fisherman at heart, huh?"

"He hates beef and gets a rash with chicken. I don't know if he's had fish before."

"Is that why all of the main dish baby foods are either lamb or turkey?"

"Yes. I told you that on the supply list."

"Wendy, I'm trying. Admittedly, I haven't tried hard enough, but from here on out, I'll give it my all."

Her face pulled taut. "Too little, too late."

"What's that supposed to mean?"

"It's convenient for you to come to this great revelation this late in the game." She set down her glass and started to mangle the salmon with agitated stabs from her fork.

"Hey—I know you're upset with me—"

"Don't chalk it up to that, Ben. I understand you were upset and spoke out of turn. I've done plenty of that myself. That's forgiven and forgotten."

"Then—"

She shot him a silencing look. "You just admitted you haven't tried hard enough to learn about Troy's care. With only Thursday and Friday to go, you'll probably dig in with notable enthusiasm and zeal, and then Saturday will dawn. I have this terrible feeling I'll wake up to a bunch of boxes you've packed during the night, and you'll give me that I-gave-it-my-best-shot look and tell me in all earnestness that you're simply not competent to handle Troy."

"Wendy!"

"Oh, give me a break," she snapped impatiently. "Even if you plow in and give it everything you've got, you're not going to have any confidence two days from now. You haven't bothered to set up any child care arrangements, and I haven't heard you place any more orders for baby food, formula, or diapers over the radio."

She was more than right; but she was also very wrong. He'd decided to truly give the situation a chance. He'd need more time, more experience, more help. The heater clicked, then cycled. It was the only sound in the whole cabin as she glared at him. Ben whispered a desperate prayer for help, then said, "So stay here another week."

eight

Her fork clattered to the plate. "I have to go back home!"

"Why not stay a little while longer? If you do, I'll have a chance to get to know Troy better, to figure out if I'm able to care for him and suited to being his guardian."

"Unh-unh! Come Saturday, I'm getting on Howie's plane and getting out of here."

"Why?" He scowled. "You don't have anyone waiting for you."

She balled up her napkin and tossed it down on the table. As she struggled to her feet, she continued, "My job is important to me."

He winced. "I didn't mean—"

"Yes, you did. I've put my life on hold because I loved Laura and want the best for her baby. My boss was irritated with me—several times. I've called in sick because I couldn't arrange child care. I can only imagine what he said when Bruce told him I got stranded up here."

"What about Troy?"

"Ben." She pressed her hand to her forehead in agitation and anguish. "He's your responsibility. Our bargain was that you'd really try to learn and I'd be a resource for you. This was supposed to be a true team effort. You have put forth some effort, but not enough—and we both know it. I've put my heart and soul into caring for him for five-and-a-half weeks, and you've barely given him five-and-a-half days."

"Fine. Then don't do a thing for him," he flung back at her, rising abruptly. His thigh hit the table and their glasses both tumbled over. Their sodas ran over the smooth wood and flooded the front of her robe.

She stepped back and let out a distraught cry.

"I thought you didn't mind being wet," he quoted her in a bitter tone.

"I don't have anything to wear!"

"It's not a big deal. Settle down." He pushed past her and opened his closet. He impatiently jerked a flannel shirt from the hanger, held it up, and looked over it at her. He stuffed it back on the hanger and pulled out another that might have been slightly smaller. "All of my stuff is too big for you. You'll swim in it, but at least this will work for a nightie. Go take your shower. Just pass me the wet stuff so I can get it going in the laundry with your other clothes."

Troy started to fuss while Wendy took a shower. Ben took a deep breath and muttered to himself, "Dive in, Hawthorne. The kid's in your hands." He changed Troy's diaper and stuffed a pacifier in his face. The supply of jarred baby food was getting low. Two unopened cans of formula powder sat on a kitchen shelf, and one more looked about half full. It occurred to him that he didn't even know how long a can lasted. He needed both hands to operate the type on the computer, so he tried putting Troy in the sling. Troy kicked up a ruckus, so Ben dragged the chair over by the desk, stuck him in it, and tied him there with a dish towel.

Unsure of what was required, Ben took a wild stab at ordering necessities for Troy. Ben used Wendy's supply list of items and quantities—but he wasn't sure whether the figures were for a week or a month. By the time he signed off, he was flummoxed. Had he ordered enough diapers? He probably should have asked Wendy how many Troy went through each day, but he felt reticent to ask her much of anything just now. He should have asked that days ago. At least he knew Troy used five jars of food and one of juice each day—but Wendy put a case of each flavor of baby food, and he didn't know how many jars were in a case.

Troy gave up on gnawing on his little giraffe and demanded attention. Ben gave him a fistful of Cheerios, but instead of eating them, Troy started throwing them. "Oh, boy. How has she managed you?" Ben grumbled under his breath.

A short while later, Troy's cooperation level hit an all-time low when confronted with his creamed spinach. Ben studied the contents of the jar, and his nose wrinkled in disgust. "I don't blame you, Buddy. This looks really bad and smells rotten."

"He needs the iron. He's not good about eating meat."

At least she's still talking to me, he thought as he turned toward the bathroom door where she stood. Forcing his voice to sound neutral, he asked, "What do I do about it, then?"

"I've been giving him baby vitamins." She tried hard to keep the impatience out of her voice. At least Ben had tried to feed Troy while she got cleaned up.

The washing machine stopped cycling, and she made a beeline for the laundry room. She'd never felt so conspicuous in her life. Ben's extra-long shirt covered clear down past her knees, but they both knew it was his. The flannel felt soft, but the way that warm softness brushed her skin felt like a never-ending hug.

"I'll get the clothes, Wendy. Curl up on the sofa and cover up with a blanket. I'll get you a robe in a jiffy." Giving her a roguish smile, he shrugged. "That shirt never looked so good."

"Neither has that sling," she countered, giving him a once-over.

He glanced down. "I forgot I had it on. I like the way the backpack carrier works better. I'm even more interested in having some extra newfangled gear sent up for Troy now that I've tried it. I went on-line and started looking at some of the stuff they make. Maybe you could give me your opinion."

"I'm not much farther along the path, Ben. All of the baby gear is new to me too." She headed back to her room.

"Stay on out here awhile," he invited. "I think we ought to try to talk things out."

She froze but didn't turn around. "Ben, please stop focusing on things and concentrate on Troy. He'll survive without another carrier or toy—what he needs is you to sign the papers and make him your own."

"I am not what he needs, Wendy."

Loose curls almost obscured her face as she dipped her head. "I can't give Troy what he needs. It hurts to say that, but I can't handle things anymore. I'm single too. I work crazy hours, weekends, and holidays, so Bruce and I scrambled every day just to be sure Troy wasn't left alone. Bruce is seriously dating a gal—"

"Would they take Troy?"

"No. She's a widow and has four kids already. Face it, Ben: I can't solve this problem. I can't take care of Troy. End of matter."

"Hasn't it crossed your mind that it might be hard for me to admit that I'm not able to care for him either?"

Finally, she lifted her face to his. Her eyes sparkled with tears. Her hands fisted at her sides. "No, it hasn't. From the first moment, you've disavowed any responsibility."

"Hey—you shocked me, bringing him here!"

"I know I shocked you, Ben. Even so, you're already picking up the skills you need—"

"I'm not close to being capable."

"You're feeding him, making bottles, changing him. I know it's a challenge, and I just went through it with him myself. There are days when it all feels overwhelming."

"There's an understatement."

She drew in a slow, deep breath. "I know we have a problem. Really, it's your problem, because Laura made you Troy's guardian. I'm trying my best to help you get on your feet, so please stop trying to bail out. I can't rescue you—you need to adjust."

"Wendy, I don't plan to adjust. If you truly won't take Troy, at least help me find a good home for him."

"What makes you think I'm any better at figuring out where he should go?"

"I know that you truly care for him." Ben approached her slowly. He verbally ticked off his points. "He's in good shape and seems happy enough. You went through a lot of trouble on his behalf to track me down and then outfitted him for this climate and brought along extra supplies to get him off on a good start. I've seen the sweet look you wear when you cuddle him."

"Stop! This is starting to sound suspiciously like a segue into a you-keep-him sales job."

His reproachful look and abrasive, "It wasn't meant to be that," only added to the tension between them. "I just asked for help, trying to get him situated."

"I'm going to bed. Arguing won't accomplish anything." She folded her arms across her ribs and left for her room without a backward glance. She didn't emerge again until the next morning.

&

"Wendy, Troy's sick," Ben stated without preamble when she appeared. "He's got a nasty rash all over."

Pushing her hand through untamed curls, she hurried toward them. "Does he have a fever? Let me take a look."

She recognized the problem at once. "Hives. He did the same thing with chicken. The doctor had me give him some stuff. I brought it along just in case. It's listed on the sheet I included on all of his allergies." She went to the cabinet and pulled out a bottle filled with clear, pink fluid. "The dosage is by weight. He's thirteen pounds."

"So he's really okay?"

"Yes. He itches, though. Bathe him in baking soda water and give him more fluid today."

"What do you think did it?" Ben gently caressed Troy's downy hair and back. "I don't want to put him through this again."

"I'd guess that it was probably the salmon. He didn't have anything else new or different yesterday, did he?"

"No, all he had was formula and baby food. I feel so bad for doing this to him."

She kept her eyes trained on Troy. "I know how you feel. I

cried when the chicken I fed him did this too. The pediatrician's only consolation was that babies don't remember all of the mistakes you make early on. Try to remember that."

"That's a nice thought. Your clothes are over on the coffee table. Since you think Troy's all right, we'll go into town and get you a few more things to wear. The diner makes good flapjacks, so we'll eat out."

It didn't take Wendy long to get ready, but when she reappeared in the living room with the suitcase in her hand, their departure stalled. Ben scowled at her. "I know things aren't great between us, but you don't have to run away."

"I'm doing what I think is best."

"Wendy, you don't understand. The Rivians own the store. Their daughter runs the diner. It's really one tiny partitioned building, and they live in it too. There's a small hall we use for town meetings, church, weddings, and the like. We don't even heat it most of the time. Susan Blossom has a one-room cabin. She does postal business and coordinates home schooling.

"Eight of us work the pump station," Ben continued, "and we're all fairly close to it. I snowmobile to it each morning, and during blizzards, it's set up and stocked so we can camp there. Three of the other pump station workers are married and have families, and you've met Harry, Cletus, and Gil."

Hope flickered in the depths of her eyes. "I know. I could go cook for them."

"No!" he cut in. His face darkened with fury. "Their whole place is half this size, and it's a pig sty."

"I could clean it."

"You shouldn't have to earn your keep," he practically roared.

"You don't have any room to speak—it's a good thing I love Troy and was willing to stay, because you practically tried to blackmail me into baby-sitting him!"

Ben gritted his teeth. "This is different. I was totally helpless and clueless. Those men can easily fend for themselves. Close quarters there would be unsafe. Wendy, they don't even have a door on the bathroom."

She winced. He pressed his advantage by continuing to recite the features making all of the other homes unsuitable. "The other station worker is a bachelor who knocked together a cabin that's so cold, he's had to give up and live with the Perns for this winter."

"There have to be others."

"The Seal twins are research scientists who live off a ways, but they're so overrun with equipment, they sleep in bunk beds to save space. Three other families have three generations under the same roof, one even has four. No one has extra space."

"Isn't there anyone else?" she asked in a small, tight voice.

He shook his head. "We're a small community that joined the native settlement when the pipeline went through. No one makes any pretenses that they have anything more than the simple necessities, and we like being rugged individualists without a lot of the extra trappings or status symbols."

"What if I pay to heat the hall? Could I stay there, then?"

"Wendy, you don't have to feel this desperate."

"Don't tell me how to feel."

He sighed and studied at her for a long moment. She looked ready to shatter. He owed her an explanation. Purposefully, he gentled his voice. "It takes thirty-six hours to get the heat on and warm up the hall, Wendy. It has no bathing facilities. By the time it's warm enough for you to stay in, you'll be leaving."

"Why couldn't you have been married and lived some place normal?" she wailed.

❧

The trip into town in a borrowed four-wheel-drive truck confirmed everything Ben had said. The minute they stepped into the store, someone called out, "Ben, I almost called you this morning. My brother and his friend want to come up in the spring to fish. Can they stay with you again?"

"Sure. Tell them to bring their sleeping bags, though." He

paused for a second and added, "I promised Janet that her sister's family could come in the spring too. They asked for late May."

"I'll get back to you with a date."

"Fine." He readjusted his hold on Troy and headed for the bookshelf stacked high with several folded garments. Clearly, this was the store's entire selection of clothing.

Following in his wake, Wendy looked around and felt a wave of bleakness wash over her. Her dim hope for a reprieve was completely, cruelly extinguished.

"Here, this ought to do the trick." Ben located a thick, pale blue turtleneck and tucked the top of the garment under his chin as he fumbled to unfold it for her inspection. "They have a few sweatshirts, if you think they might be a little warmer."

"I don't care."

Her voice was thick with tears, and he knew why. She loved Troy—she'd admitted it flat out; but she felt so sure she couldn't keep him, she'd finally hit the point of trying to separate for the sake of self-preservation. No matter what he'd said, she'd harbored a small hope of finding a way to move out, and that hope had been extinguished like a candle in a flame.

Ben pleated the turtleneck in one hand and laid it over her shoulder. The action allowed him to gently run his hand across her shoulder and down her arm. He rumbled under his breath, "Wendy, these people aren't going to understand if you break down in here. This is their life, their home. When we leave, you can sit in the truck and sob like a baby, but please, not in here."

She nodded and bit her lower lip to regain her composure.

Everyone acted warm and friendly, as the others had when they'd come to visit her at Ben's place. They admired Troy, fretted over his hives, and wondered what Wendy thought of Alaska. Ben smoothly answered, "She thinks it's cold. Howie got his wires crossed and sent her a copy of his normal schedule. He forgot to mention that he was going to take a week off.

She thought she'd be going home right away, so she didn't come equipped for our weather."

Madeline Rivian promptly insisted upon raiding her own closet and provided a snowsuit she claimed was too small for her anymore. She also donated a warm wool sweater. Her daughter, Diane, threw in a sweatsuit and a pair of leggings. Their offhanded kindness made Wendy think of how incredibly hospitable everyone had been since she'd arrived in Caribou Crossing.

Ben cruised around the small store. He eyed Wendy critically to measure her, then grabbed a set of thermal long johns, another pair of sweats, and a package of socks. He discreetly turned away while Wendy grabbed a few necessities, but when she opened her purse to get out her wallet, he cut her off at the pass. "Just put it on my account, Madeline. I need eggs, milk, and bread. We're going to have breakfast next door, so I'll just sweep back in to get them before we leave."

"You can't buy my stuff," Wendy hissed.

He cocked a brow that dared her to say anything more.

"Is something wrong?" Madeline asked.

"No." Ben lifted his chin imperiously. "I think we're set."

Madeline let out a tinkling laugh. "I know that look, Ben. I'll put it on your tab. Oh, one more thing: My Lisa is due any time now. I'll fly out to be with her for a month or so. You might want to take one more look around, because Sam won't keep the store open much while I'm gone."

"I got you." He wandered around with Troy nestled in the crook of one arm and added several things to his pile on the counter. After evaluating it, he mumbled under his breath and tossed on a few more items for good measure. "I think that ought to do."

"Thanks for understanding. I just have to go be with her. I wish she'd come back, you know."

Ben nodded. He clued Wendy in. "Lisa's husband left her. She's all by herself in Wisconsin. Madeline promised to go help her out with the baby until she has things squared away."

Wendy's eyes shone with compassion. "Lisa is lucky to have you, Mrs. Rivian."

"Madeline, Dear. Thank you, and enjoy your breakfast."

As they finished eating breakfast in the diner, Harry and Gil stomped in. Wendy noted everyone made a habit of scraping snow and ice off outside, and though it was sensible and thoughtful, it made her feel like she was surrounded by a herd of clumsy bulls.

"Hey! Lookie who's here." Harry strode over, flipped a chair around backward, and straddled it. He scooted closer to Wendy. She politely inched her chair to the side to make room, but when he drew close enough to brush arms, she leaned away even more.

Gil joined them. Red-faced, he mumbled a nearly unintelligible greeting. Harry kicked the other chair out for him, so he sidled in. "The usual?" Diane called over from the counter.

"Yep," came the duet.

"So how are you doing?" Harry grinned at Wendy. He inhaled deeply, closed his eyes, and added, "I'm doing mighty fine today. One sniff of that perfume you're wearing could make a man's whole day."

Wendy busied herself offering Troy a sip of apple juice. When she glanced up, she expected to see Ben's taunting you-wanted-to-go-stay-with-him look.

Instead, Ben gulped the last of his orange juice and thrust his chair away from the table. "We're fine, and what you're smelling is Troy's diaper. Wendy, perhaps Diane could let you look through the medical supplies to see if they have vitamins for the baby since I didn't order any."

"No need to hurry away," Gil mumbled.

Wendy shook her head. "Really. It's nothing personal. The baby has hives, so I want him home so we can unbundle him a bit."

"Poor tyke." Gil frowned. "Do you have calamine?"

"Yes," Ben snapped as he pulled Wendy over toward his side of the table, away from Harry.

Harry looked at them and rubbed his jaw. "You up for some. . .poker tonight?"

"No." Ben's voice was stern, his expression unyielding. "We need to watch the baby. Wendy and I will be reviewing all of the particulars so I'll be capable later on."

"When I leave," she tacked on.

"Okay. If you think more about my proposition," Harry tempted, "just write."

Ben dragged Wendy through the store. The Rivians went out to load the groceries into the truck for him as he stuffed Wendy into her borrowed coat. He rasped in an increasingly surly tone, "Wendy, you can't flirt or be coy. Harry's a rough man. Good, but barely civilized. Tell him to hush up and leave you alone. He's got rocks in his head for thinking you'd ever want to be his mail-order bride."

Her jaw dropped. "How did you know?"

"The idiot's been shooting his mouth off at the pumping station and to anyone else who'll listen. Do yourself and everyone else a favor—tell him straight up that you're not interested."

"I did."

He groaned.

So did she.

"Let's get out of here."

An uneasy peace hovered between Ben and Wendy for the remainder of the day. He'd arranged with one of the women to start watching Troy on Wednesday and mentioned that he had supplies coming in on the Saturday plane, so it was clear he would keep the boy—at least for the immediate future.

While he was at work on Friday, Wendy did as much cooking as she could. It would be nice to at least leave him with some frozen meals since he'd be juggling a new and daunting set of responsibilities. He expressed his gratitude for her thoughtfulness but acted subdued.

"I know it's not easy, Ben. Still, you're all little Troy has. Really try to make it work."

He crammed his fists in his pockets and nodded. He'd never begged for anything in his life, and he wasn't going to start now, even though he felt sorely tempted to do just that. The last few days of taking over all of Troy's care had been a complete lesson in humility.

There was so much he didn't know. If she would just stay another measly week, he'd at least have more than mere feeding and diapering down. Indeed, they'd run out of diapers and were having to use the cloth ones. He'd impaled himself with the pins several times.

"I arranged with Chuck Pearson to cover for my shift tomorrow. Howie ought to get in about eleven."

She nodded.

"Wendy, I've been praying about this. I've seen you pray over Troy each night. Tonight, let's pray together."

Tears filled her eyes, but she nodded.

Troy lay fast asleep in the playpen. Ben held onto the rail with his left hand and settled his right arm around Wendy's shoulders. He sensed she was too upset to pray aloud, so he bowed his head and started in.

"Thank you," she whispered thickly when he'd finished the prayer. "I'll see you in the morning." She slipped off to her room.

Ben wasn't sure, but he thought he might have heard her crying.

The next day, Wendy fingered Troy's bunting as she waited at the landing strip. Her voice was muted, and she wouldn't look up into Ben's face. "I laundered all of the clothes Madeline and Diane lent me. Please give them my thanks. Write and let me know how he is."

"Go ahead and kiss him," Ben whispered roughly.

She shook her head and trembled, "I can't."

"Then I'll give it to him for you." He tilted her face up to his and claimed her lips. She was momentarily stunned but then wrapped her arms around them both and kissed him back. She put her heart and soul into the kiss, then tore away with a sob. Without looking back, she scrambled into the small plane and buckled up.

The engines had barely started whining when a car came up, its horn blasting in a strange pattern. Howie grumbled, "Now what?" as he unbuckled himself and climbed out.

Wendy refused to look out the window. She kept her head bowed and held her purse tightly. The door opened again, but it was Ben. "Get out of the plane."

"What?"

"Get out of the plane, Wendy!"

He fumbled with her seat belt. "Chuck Pearson fell. His leg is broken. We don't have a doctor. Howie has to fly him out of here. We have to remove your seat to make enough room. Get out!" He didn't even wait for her to comply. He unlinked the belt. As the webbing snaked back into the holder, he scooped her up and pulled her out of the seat.

Ten minutes later, the plane took off. Wendy sat in the passenger seat of the Jeep, wrapped her arms around Troy, and wept.

Part of Ben was elated for the brief reprieve, but the cost was too high. Chuck's broken leg and Wendy's unhappiness were both enough to make Ben feel slightly sick to his stomach. He slid into the driver's seat and silently passed her his handkerchief. As they took the icy road back home, the crib and the baby things Howie had delivered rattled in the back of the battered Jeep—the only accompaniment to her muffled sobs. When her weeping waned, he attempted to soothe her by promising, "Howie will come back on Tuesday."

She sniffled and gave him a watery smile. "Remember when Abraham found the ram in the thicket so he didn't have to sacrifice Isaac? God isn't giving Troy to me, but He's letting me have a little more time." She bit her lip, then sighed. "I just hope my boss understands."

Once they got back to the cabin, Ben carried things into the house and dumped them into the living room. Wendy started unbundling Troy when he cleared his throat and informed her in an apologetic voice, "Chuck was covering at work for me. I have to go to the pumping station. Leave everything alone. I'll unpack things this evening."

Her nose had turned red from crying and her eyes, bloodshot. Every speck of color had left her cheeks, and her hair looked like she'd stirred the curls with a stick. Ben knew he wanted her to stay there—not just for a few more nights, but forever. He looked past the temporary ravages of her crying and thought she was beautiful. Brushing her hair behind her ear with the backs of his fingers in a gentle caress, he whispered, "Starting tomorrow, Lael will come to watch Troy, but for now, I need to ask you to keep an eye on him for me."

"Of course I will."

"I know it nearly broke your heart to leave him."

She looked at him, her eyes shining like emeralds through the tears that welled up. "It did. I don't know what to do."

"We have a few days to talk and pray."

Snow fell heavily when Ben got home. Wendy sat curled up on the couch, sipping what smelled like hot cocoa. As soon as he peeled out of his warm parka and boots, he paced across the room and sat in one of the corduroy chairs. "I called your brother to tell him you got bumped from your flight."

"Thank you."

He couldn't stand the distance between them any longer. He rose and stood behind her. Gently kneading the terrible tension in her shoulders, he praised, "You've been a trooper, Wendy. I'll continue to take care of Troy at night, and Lael will be here tomorrow."

"It's silly for her to come."

"Not really. I think you'll enjoy her company. She's a nice lady. She knits like a house afire, though. Most of the women here do."

"That just proves," she moaned as he hit a kink and rubbed it out, "I don't belong here."

"You don't knit?"

"By the time I'm done with a ball of yarn, even a kitten won't play with it."

"Good." He chuckled. "I hate watching a woman clack those needles. It throws my conversation and thought process off. Laura's mom knitted, and she dragged a hideous-looking bag with her wherever she went so she wouldn't waste any valuable time without those stupid needles going."

"That's funny. Laura didn't make anything for Troy. I'd think her mother must have taught her how."

"Nope. She and I were co-conspirators. We'd actually hide the knitting bag or her yarn to get some respite. If Troy had anything that was knitted, it was supplied as a gift."

"Speaking of supplies, you have a fair load of them." Wendy swept her hand across the room. The jerky gesture reinforced the tension singing through her. She drew in a long, shaky breath, then shivered. "I thought I'd put them away for you, but decided not to. You need to know what you have and where it is."

"I'll get to them after awhile. Go on ahead and slip in for a shower. I'll heat up some soup."

She twisted sideways on the couch and rested her cheek on the back of a cushion. "I thought we'd just microwave one of those things I froze."

"Fine by me." He stopped massaging her and threw one of Troy's blankets over her coiled form. As he walked toward the kitchen, he asked, "Any special requests?"

"I don't care."

A short while later, he tenderly drew circles on her temple. "Sweetie, chow's on. Want to eat at the table, or would you rather stay put and have it here?"

"I don't care."

Finger combing her hair, he decided, "Stay put. I'll light a quick fire, and it'll be real cozy."

Troy babbled happily and scooted across the floor on his bottom while the adults ate. "Whoa, Buster." Ben hopped up and grabbed Troy as he got close to the hearth. "He's moving a lot faster than he was just two days ago."

Wendy nodded.

Ben set Troy down all of the way across the room, then put his plate on the coffee table so he would be in the boy's path toward the fireplace. Troy kicked and scooted his way across the floor several times, and it was obvious that he did it on purpose to draw closer to Ben. Finally Ben set him on his lap and let him play with the spoon.

Wendy cleared her throat. "I spent time in the Word today. Ben, when I had to give up my seat on the plane, I hoped so much it was God's way of telling me Troy was mine." A tear streaked down her cheek, and she pushed it away with a shaky hand. "Before you came home, I had an overwhelming sense that Troy belongs with you. I tried to deny it, but look at the two of you. He's bonding with you, crawls to you, wants you." Her voice broke. "Laura sensed her son should come to you. She was right."

The fire caught and crackled cheerfully. Under other circumstances, it could have been a delightful situation. As things stood, Ben sensed Wendy's emotional turmoil and respected it by refraining from pushing her to carry on a conversation. The tumult in her eyes made his heart ache.

Ben collected her plate and refrained from mentioning she'd barely eaten half of the meal. Instead of offering to wash or dry the dishes as she usually did, she stayed curled up on the couch and stared at the fire. Just as Ben finished cleaning the kitchen, Troy started to make a fuss.

"I recognize that one. It's his I'm-a-hungry-little-beast noise. What should I feed him? His usual meat and veggies?"

"Yes."

Balancing Troy on his lap, Ben commented, "Your highchair came today, Buster. Maybe we won't be so messy if I have both hands free. Hmm. How did I miss noticing this?" He patted Troy's bottom. "Looks like you're back in disposable diapers."

"I think I'll go to bed."

"Not yet, Wendy. You're all comfy where you are, and I'm busy with Troy. Besides, the fire feels good. Stay put and relax."

She sagged into the cushions of the sofa.

"There's my girl," he murmured approvingly. He leaned forward, pressed a gentle kiss onto her forehead, and got up. "I'll set the high chair so you can get a kick out of Troy's eating antics. The kid is an absolute pig."

Two hours later, Ben pulled down the bedclothes in the spare room and rubbed his bristly face. He'd put away all of the new supplies. Troy was a delightful companion for the process. He even pulled himself into a standing position by hanging onto Ben's jeans.

A bittersweet smile twisted Wendy's face as she watched it happen. After that, she'd lain on the couch and stayed eerily silent. She'd eventually fallen asleep.

She stirred restlessly in Ben's arms as he carried her to bed. He made a few soft sounds to soothe her. Not wanting to let go, Ben sat on her bed for a few minutes and buried his face in her curls. Her hair felt almost as soft as Troy's. He had to smile. It smelled of baby shampoo.

It was just as well that it did. The fragrance smelled so distinct, it put a damper on the burgeoning attraction he felt. His heart ached as he tucked her in and walked away. She'd be staying with him just a few more days. . .and he didn't know how he'd be able to let her go again.

❧

A strange woman greeted Wendy when she woke up the next morning. "Hi! I'm Lael. Ben told me to let you sleep in late. Troy's a cute little boy. I can't believe Ben bought bananas. Have one."

The woman's conversation was like buckshot—scattering and covering everything all at once. Wendy blinked for a moment before she remembered her manners. "It's nice to meet you, Lael. I don't particularly care for bananas. Thank you anyway."

"Oh. I thought everyone loved them. They're terribly expensive, you know. Everything up here is. My husband and I go to Fairbanks twice a year just to stock up on a bunch of stuff. I don't think we'll be able to do that this year because Howie's the only pilot available. It really has cut down on what we can all do."

"I noticed that," was the wry retort.

Lael merely giggled and picked up knitting needles. "Get your breakfast and come sit. I'm making a sweater. Do you knit?"

"Not at all."

"Oh." She looked nonplused for a moment, then brightened. "Ben said you like to cook, so I brought cookbooks for you to read. I'm going to feed Troy his breakfast. Ben's list says he's supposed to have oatmeal and pears."

By the time she left, Lael had fed Troy all three of his meals and cheerfully imparted, "I've made his bottles for the nighttime. I'll see you tomorrow."

"You look worlds better today," Ben stated quietly to Wendy as soon as Lael left and they sat down to eat.

"I actually took a nap today."

He grinned. "Good. Did you get along okay with Lael?"

"Just as soon as I convinced her that I shouldn't try to knit or eat bananas."

"You don't like bananas?"

"Never have." She shuddered. "They're too mushy."

"They're a delicacy up here. Mango, guava, nectarines, apricots—all of those things are like hen's teeth. I paid five bucks for a basket of strawberries my first spring up here because I was so desperate to have them."

"Five dollars!"

"Best five bucks I ever spent." He subconsciously licked his lips, as if he could still taste the sweetness. "I got smart, though. There's a fruit-of-the-month club where they send you something each month. They weren't thrilled when I subscribed, but when I enrolled everyone in Caribou Crossing as my Christmas gift, the shipping costs to the company dropped significantly. They have a standard crate booked each month on the plane, and everyone knows just when to expect it."

"What month do strawberries come?"

"May," he shot back without a moment's hesitation. "June is peaches."

"Don't they get pretty battered?"

He shook his head. "They're packaged with remarkable care, and Howie flies them in with eggs, so he takes special pains with the landing."

"Don't you itch to go to a real grocery store and fill up a cart with anything that strikes your fancy?"

He admitted, "I do that several times a year. You wouldn't ask that if you'd been up in the attic. Since it's cool and dry, nothing goes stale. I have everything from animal cookies to Zagnut candy bars."

"Iced animal cookies? The pink-and-white ones?"

Chortling softly, he nodded. "I can see it's time for you to climb the stairs to heaven." He popped Troy into the playpen and half-dragged Wendy up to the attic.

She stood and gaped at the overflowing shelves. "Wow! Look at this place."

"Yeah. I get all of my staples as a routine order through the Rivians. All of my chicken and beef comes from their store. Bread and eggs and milk—you know. The rest of the stuff I fly in like I did with Troy's baby stuff. There's a company in Fairbanks that takes a computer order and shops for me. Here are those cookies you wanted."

"I can't eat them."

"Sure you can." He put them in her hand. "I'll share them. We even have milk to go with them."

"Why do you have these cans of milk?"

"I hate powdered milk. If I'm snowed in, adding water to evaporated milk tastes better than nothing at all."

"Snowed in?" her voice cracked.

"Yes, Wendy. It's part and parcel of living up here. I make

sure I have plenty of stuff in case I'm stranded. Lael and I have an understanding. If I'm at work when a blizzard hits, she'll stay here with Troy, so you don't need to worry. Her husband doesn't mind."

"What does he do?"

"He and the Packards run a hunting/fishing/photography tour business. They started it four years ago, and it's grown more each year. This spring, they're going to put up guest cabins."

"Ordered from the log cabin company?"

He tapped her nose playfully. "You're learning, Cookie." His smile melted at once. "I'm sorry. You asked me to stop calling you that."

The side of her mouth crooked upward. "First impressions are lasting, aren't they?"

"In your case, mine sure have been. What about you?"

"Might be."

"That's pretty cryptic."

Wendy gave him a dainty shrug.

"So? 'Fess up. What was your first impression?"

"You thought I was a cook; I thought you were huge."

"That's the abbreviated form." He helped her down the stairs and closed the latch. "I got one look at you and thought that you have stunning eyes. You were stirring the stew, and your hips swayed with the action. You're a beautiful woman."

"Right," she drawled mockingly.

"Why can't you stop putting yourself down?"

"I don't believe in flattery."

"Neither do I. I don't like skinny women. Beanpoles just don't do anything for me. You're trim, but there's enough of you to appreciate, and I'm not afraid you'll break if I hug you. Now I'll either start hugging you, or you can tell me what your first impressions of me were. What's your choice?"

"I'm going to give Troy his vitamins."

"So you can't do that and converse at the same time?"

She gave him a wide-eyed look. "No, I can't. Absolutely,

positively cannot. It's too hard to divide my attention between two tasks."

"So you can't walk and chew bubble gum at the same time?"

"Nope," she agreed breezily. "I'm appallingly uncoordinated and clumsy."

After Troy swallowed his vitamins, they stood side by side at the sink and bathed him. "I like this part of the evening," Ben said. "Lael offered to bathe him, but I like watching him splash. I always wondered what experts meant when they tossed out the phrase 'family time,' but I get the idea now."

"And just what do you think I am?"

"Family."

"I take back what I said, Hawthorne." She nudged his hip with hers and laughed. "It's a good thing you haven't become a father. Uncle is fine, father is completely out of the picture. I understand several forms of insanity are hereditary, and I'm afraid you exhibit several of the hallmarks of being certifiable."

nine

She emerged from the shower to find Ben lying on his belly on the floor. He and Troy gleefully babbled to one another. Wendy couldn't help grinning. "He's so cute, isn't he?"

"Yep. Noisy too." Ben got up and swept Troy into the playpen. "Let me square him away." He slipped the giraffe into the baby's small hand, deftly tucked the blanket up to his neck, then stalked over and shoved something into Wendy's mouth.

"What is this?"

He stood in front of her and curled his hands around her hips in a secure hold. "Bubble gum. You said you can't chew gum and walk at the same time. Time to learn, Sweetie."

She glanced down at her thick chenille robe and flannel nightgown in disbelief. "I'm supposed to take lessons in this get up?"

His boyish grin was pure cheesecake. "I'll take you however you come."

"I'm going to stomp on your feet!"

"Is that a threat, or are you warning me you're really horribly clumsy?"

"Both."

He let out an entertained chuckle and exerted quick pressure on her hips. His action swiveled her around so he stood behind her. "Here we go now. Chew, step, chew, step, chew, step. There you go."

"You're impossible." She giggled. Every move made her knee bump her forward, forcing her to walk in cadence to his silly instructions.

He wrapped his arms around her and rumbled, "You're a lot of fun, Wendy."

"I thought you said I was nothing but tr—"

He pulled her into a sudden, dramatic dip and stopped the word with an almost-kiss. His mouth barely hovered above her lips. "Don't you say that. It's not fair to quote a man when he's pushed beyond the realm of endurance."

She had to cling to him or fall. There was no way to right herself. Wendy knotted his shirt in both hands as she tried to steady herself and her breathing at the same time. "You have me off balance again."

He chuckled. "So I do." He brought her back up, then pried her mouth open with his fingers.

She batted his hand away. "What are you doing?"

Nodding his head in satisfaction, he commented, "Yep, the gum's still there. We're ready to move on to Step Two."

"Step Two?"

"Step Two: Dancing while chewing gum."

"I thought you just tried Step Two."

"Kissing? Unh-unh. That was no kiss, and we both know it. I don't steal kisses, Wendy—they're something special to be shared. I'm more than happy to progress to that stage if you're interested, though."

"That's an offer I'll have to resist."

With complete melodramatic flair, he exclaimed, "Foiled again!"

"Again? Just how many women do you try to romance?"

"You're asking that, standing in the middle of a frozen tundra? The total population of Caribou Crossing doesn't hit three digits. You're the sweetest surprise Howie ever hauled up here, and I'm standing first in line to snap you up! Here. Let's dance."

"I don't dance. Never have."

"Good. You won't know how truly awful and out-of-practice I am."

She gave him a wary look, then glanced down at her feet. "I don't think this is a good idea."

"Being close, or risking your feet?"

"Both!"

He chuckled. "Honey, believe me: This is only for fun. If I were trying to seduce you, I'd never suggest dancing."

"So I could be a hunchbacked Cyclops, and you'd still want to dance?"

He pretended to give the question grave consideration and queried, "Would that eye still be beguiling green?"

"Ben, there isn't enough room to dance in here."

"Sure there is. Now remember not to bite your tongue as you chew that gum."

As she giggled, he reached around her and hit a button on his sound system. After he fiddled with another button, a polka came on. He grabbed her hands, stepped backward a full twelve inches, and ordered, "C'mon and follow me. Heel, toe, heel, toe, slide, slide, slide."

"Ben?"

"Hmmm?"

"I can see why you're still single."

A short while later, she changed Troy and was ready to dash off to the privacy of her bedroom when Ben handed her a cup of cocoa. "Sit back down and relax. I gave you a real workout."

Bobbing her head in seemingly complete assent, she put on a mock serious expression. "Indeed. Doing the polka in a flannel nightgown is likely to strain something—most likely the imagination."

"Not exactly, but then again, it was fun." His eyes lit with pleasure. "Since you brought up imagination, tell me about your dreams for the future. What is it that you want?"

She slid away from him and settled into the farthest corner of the couch. After taking a sip of the cocoa, she ventured, "You know I'm a Christian. My biggest goal is to walk with Christ. After that, I want to continue to cook, I guess."

"What about a husband and children?"

Her hands tightened around the mug, and pain clutched her heart. Why did he have to bring that up?

"I'm not trying to be insensitive, Wendy. You might find a widower with children, or you might adopt."

"It'll take a lot before I trust a man enough to get engaged again."

"I can't blame you for being wary, but don't you think God has a man for you?"

"I thought the first guy was the one." She bowed her head. "Obviously, my judgment was way off the mark when I got involved with someone who wasn't a Christian." Anguish struck her again as she repeated Larry's cruel words, "No man wants a wife who's not a full woman."

"Having a child doesn't make you a woman; it makes you a mother. You're already a woman—a very warm, special—"

She set the mug down abruptly. "Please stop. I know that's true, but I always wanted kids. Listen. I don't want to talk about this anymore. . .about me anymore." She took a deep breath and let it out slowly. "I'd rather have you tell me what you want for Troy."

"I've been thinking about that." He checked on Troy and leaned over to tug a satin-edged blanket from beneath his footed sleeper and drew it up to his neck. Then Ben slowly crossed the room and sat on the couch—not close enough to touch but easily within reach. His moves were as laconic as his voice. "We do church once a month up here, so I know I'll need to be even more diligent about teaching him about the Lord and reading Bible stories. As far as education, Troy'll do school by computer and video correspondence. He'll be able to hunt, trap, and cross country ski with me."

She let some of the awful tension drain away. Ben had been kind enough to honor her request and change the subject. Since they could both run with this topic, she felt safe again. "So Troy will be your pal and keep you company while you do the things you like."

"Yeah, I guess that's about the size of it." He swept his hand in a gesture that encompassed the bookshelves. "In case you didn't notice, this place is full of books. I love to read, so I'd want him to as well."

"I thought maybe you housed the local library."

"Caribou Crossing doesn't boast a library. We all have an understanding. Whenever you're a guest, it's perfectly acceptable, if not actually expected, for you to scan the books and borrow from your neighbor. Same with music and movies. Since we're isolated, we resort to simple forms of entertainment."

"Like doing the pajama polka?"

"Tonight was a first for that one. I thought it turned out to be a raging success. What about you?"

"I still chewed the bubble gum, didn't I?"

He scooted closer and tipped her head over onto his shoulder. "You have a quirky sense of humor."

"You started it!"

He grinned down at her. "You sound like a nine year old."

"Tonight has turned into a pajama party just like ones I went to when I was nine. I worry about the isolation here, about the lack of opportunities. Will Troy have playmates?"

He placed a kiss on her hair. "Chuck and Janet are expecting a son, so Troy and he'll probably be best buddies. The Perns have a granddaughter, Annie, who's about a year old, and there are a handful of other little squirts. I like the idea of Troy learning to get along with folks of all ages. It'll build character."

"If he grows up in your shadow, he'll be a character, all right."

"If? Are you starting to doubt the arrangement?"

"No, I'm not starting to hold doubts. I've had them all along." Her hands knotted in her lap. "I think you'll do well with him. I just don't know if you show the attitude and confidence it takes. Never once have you said you'll keep him."

"Look at it from my perspective, Wendy. A stepsister I haven't connected with for years willed me a nephew I didn't know existed. Until you staged this surprise drop off, I'd never even held a baby."

"I guessed that. You acted like I'd shoved a live grenade into your arms."

"I've gotten better."

"You're a pro now."

"Yeah, well, I still don't know how I'm supposed to rear him. My dad was an absentee father. He worked two jobs and parked me with whichever woman inhabited the place. Some were girlfriends, three were wives. In the end, I was glad to go to college just to get away from the craziness under his roof. In fact, I had someone try to take me to court on a paternity case, but I finally figured out that my father never told her he and I shared the same name—it was his kid. I changed my name at that point so I wouldn't have to worry about being haunted by his bad choices. Still I can't help wondering—what if I'm no better?"

She cleared her throat and summoned the nerve to ask, "How many women have you had under your roof?"

"None, but that doesn't count. I'm childless—or at least I was until you pulled this little stunt."

"I wish you wouldn't blame me. I got him because Laura was a good friend and we didn't want Troy to go to a stranger in a foster home."

"I'm thankful you stepped in and took him." He slowly rubbed her shoulder and stared across the room. "I worry I won't be enough for him."

"No parent is 'enough' on his or her own," Wendy said softly. "Wisdom and patience are essential, and only God can give those qualities."

"Having Troy will certainly deepen my prayer life."

Wendy sighed. "Yeah, I know what you mean. I'm relieved to hear you say that. It's hard to let go of him, but I feel better knowing he'll be in a Christian home."

They rambled on. Ben eventually walked Wendy to her bedroom door and traced his fingers down her cheek. "You know, Sweetie, I sure like having you around."

"I'd get old real quick."

"I seriously doubt that. Why don't you slip your arms around me so I can give you a good-night kiss?"

She leaned away from him and propped her weight against the wall. Regret tainted her voice. "I won't because I'd be a fool to do that. You're a smooth talker, like to snuggle, and you have a sense of humor. Those all rank high on my list of desirable qualities, but I'm too vulnerable to allow myself to fall for anyone. I'm better off to keep some distance and remember I have life in the real world waiting for me."

He tipped her face up to his. "That man didn't know what he was giving up when he let go of you." He hesitated, then growled, "Oh, why not?" as he gently drew her close. He wrapped his arms around her in a cherishing embrace.

He had to hold Wendy for a long while before she relaxed. She fought the impulse to yield to him as long as she could. He was so faultlessly giving and gentle that her walls crumbled. His hold stayed sweet and hauntingly tender, and he finally dipped his head and said, "You're wonderfully cuddly."

Wendy breathlessly tore away when she realized she'd started to let attraction blossom. *This can't be. It's not for me. He's not for me.* Totally embarrassed and weak-kneed, she hid her face in his shirt.

He held her for a few minutes in complete, comfortable silence, then murmured, "I'd better say good night while I'm still in control. You tempt me to think about dangerous things."

Wendy went still and stared at him in dismay. "Ben, I'm sorry if I've done anything that, um. . .stirred you. I told you how I feel about permissive relation—"

His fingers pressed over her lips, effectively silencing her. "No, Cookie. I'm drawn to you, but we've both been careful to keep things chaste. I was referring to the fact that having you and Troy around tempt me to think I might actually do the family scene, after all."

Relief and joy flooded her. "Ben, especially after our talk tonight, I think you'll do a wonderful job with Troy. A family is a gift from God, and I confess, I envy you for having him."

"Is that your way of telling me you're tempted to do the family thing too?"

"You already know the answer to that. I'm tempted to sky-dive, but I'd never jump out of the plane. Some risks aren't worth the thrill."

He let out a pained chuckle.

"Sleep well, Ben."

"Pleasant dreams, Wendy."

By morning, everyone was frazzled. No one managed to get any sleep. Troy screamed all night long. He grew so loud, Wendy ventured out of her room and asked, "What's wrong?"

Ben kept pacing the floor with him and growled, "I can't tell."

"Is he running a fever?"

"No."

"It there a rash?"

"No. He's dry and full, and I don't know what to do next."

Hours later, Troy was still at it. He calmed only slightly when one of the two of them nestled him and paced the floor. When it came time for his next bottle, Wendy went to fetch it, but there weren't any more in the refrigerator. Opening the cupboard to get out the formula, she let out a squawk.

"What is it?"

"You got him the wrong stuff. He's got colic because you bought the wrong formula."

"I ordered the same kind you brought along."

Wendy looked at the ceiling and groaned. "They sent the right brand, but this one has iron."

"This is the last straw. Even when I try my hardest, I mess things up. I can't keep him."

"You gave him a royal bellyache, but he's going to live. Don't think this is an adequate excuse to bail out. The phone's working again. Just call out and get them to bring in the right stuff tomorrow. We'll use more baby food and juice for him today."

"No. Absolutely not. Wendy, you have to take him back. This isn't going to work."

"Yes, it is." She gave him a sad, sage smile and blinked back her selfish tears. "He belongs with you. I believe it with all of my heart."

A knock on the door silenced them. They hadn't even heard Lael's snowmobile. "We'll talk about this later," Wendy hissed at Ben as he got ready to leave.

"No, we won't. It's decided."

"That's what you think. I won't take him!"

Ben slammed the door shut.

❧

Saturday morning, the phone rang. Since Wendy was up to her elbows in dishwater, and Ben was arm wrestling with Troy over a spoonful of baby oatmeal, Ben hit the speakerphone button. "Hello?"

"Ben? Madeline. Lisa's had the baby."

"Congratulations! What is it?"

"A girl. She named her Kasey. She's four weeks early, so she's kind of small—five pounds, five ounces, eighteen inches long; but she's healthy."

"Wonderful! How's Lisa?"

A brief pause ensued. "That's why I'm calling. They ended up doing a cesarean, and she needs me right away. Howie's due in this afternoon."

Ben gave Wendy a searching look. She'd already packed. His expression clued Wendy into the fact that something was afoot. In a split second, she realized why Madeline must have called. She hastily dried her hands and pled, "Can't Howie fit both of us aboard?"

Madeline sighed. "I called Fairbanks. Howie already took off. He needed to take out the other seat because someone down the line had a heater break, so he wedged the replacement on board. Wendy, I hate to ask. I know you already got bumped once, but Lisa really needs me."

Ben watched her, not asking with his words, but still asking with his eyes.

Wendy's nose and eyelids tingled with the ominous burning

sensation that heralded tears. She pressed her hands to mute the sensation and nodded her head. She went back to her room and shut the door. She knelt at the bed and buried her face in the covers. *Why, Lord? Why do You keep stranding me here? Every day, it gets harder to leave Troy. Ben doesn't really need me here anymore. We're actually starting to enjoy each other—but he's getting too friendly, and I had no business letting him hold me. I already let one man break my heart, and letting go of Troy is almost more than I can bear. Please, Father, get me out of here soon!*

❧

Even though he'd never manage keeping Troy, Ben had requested different formula, and Howie delivered the right kind on the Saturday flight. Indeed, Ben had done a fine job of ordering everything Troy needed. It confirmed what Wendy already knew deep in her heart: Ben would manage just fine without her.

Monday morning, Wendy awoke to the realization that the wind had started making a different sound. Lael was already there, and she and Ben listened to the weather report with more than their usual level of interest.

"I'll make it home this evening," he determined.

"Hold it," Wendy said. "What's up?"

"A blizzard. It looks like it'll hit around eight o'clock tonight."

"It can't hit until tomorrow night. I'm leaving tomorrow afternoon."

Lael let out a trill of a laugh.

Ben touched her arm to silence her, and she stopped at once. "Jack's single and has been living with the Perns. He already volunteered to stay at the station for this one. I'll be home in time to sit it out with you. I need to go in for the day shift, though. If there's anything you'll need for the next little while, you'd better get it from the Rivians now."

In a trembling voice, Wendy demanded, "How long is a little while?"

Ben looked at her steadily, but his gaze carried an apology. "I don't know."

Lael took charge as soon as Ben left. "I drove over in my Jeep. We're going to town for breakfast. Bundle up the kid. We'll feed him at the diner. It's important to get out while we still can. I need to get some supplies too."

Allowing herself to be bullied and led, Wendy complied. Folks flocked to the diner and store, and the whole shopping trip and breakfast took on the flavor of a family reunion. Baffled, yet enchanted by everyone's genuine caring, Wendy realized the community would band together to help Ben with Troy if he ever even hinted he needed a hand. That insight felt bittersweet.

As she let the last few groceries tumble onto the Rivians' counter, Wendy wrinkled her nose. "Lael, where does Janet live? Should we take her some stuff?"

"Now isn't that the nicest thing?" Mr. Rivian chuckled. "My Diane already called Janet and put together a box for her. If you gals would drop it off, that'd be spiffy."

Janet greeted them as if they were long-lost sisters. She played with Troy for a short while, and she made a face at Wendy. "I wish you'd stay up here. We'd be great friends, and I'd love a little backup and advice once this baby of mine comes."

"Ben's planning for Troy and your son to be best friends." Wendy deftly sidestepped the issue of her staying. She didn't belong here.

A knock sounded, and the door blew open and shut. A grandmotherly woman briskly came across the room. Straps from two big bags crisscrossed her heart, but the weight in them didn't slow her down in the least. As she dumped them onto the floor, she clucked, "Janet, I should have known you'd throw a party since you couldn't get to the store. I'm staying here with you during the blizzard, and I won't hear a word otherwise."

"Wila, I'd be a fool to turn away such dear company."

Janet introduced Wendy to Wila, then handed back Troy. "You'd probably better get home. Knowing Ben, he'll go crazy if he calls and you aren't there to answer."

When they got back to Ben's cabin, Wendy thought Lael was crazy to insist that they march and cavort in the snow for awhile. After a restless lunch which they spent watching the weather report via satellite, the phone rang. Lael answered and shot Wendy a helpless look. She covered the receiver and mouthed, "It's Harry."

"Oh, no," Wendy groaned.

"Um, Harry? I'm helping Wendy get ready for the storm. . . No, no. Really. . . I'm here now, and Ben will get home before it strikes. . . . No need to worry. Thanks, anyway. G'bye." Lael ended the call and gave Wendy an apologetic wink. "He thought maybe he ought to come stay with you, but I think I kept him at bay. Harry's got a giant crush on you."

"Thanks for rescuing me. He might be a nice guy, but. . ."

"Yeah, I know. Forget it."

Less than an hour later, Wendy wished she could forget it. Harry ignored Lael's reassurances and showed up. He dragged in three huge bags. "Clothes and supplies. Lael, you can go home to your husband. A woman belongs with her man during a blizzard."

Both women tried to tell him Ben would be home in plenty of time, but Harry parked himself on the couch. From the way he settled in, it looked like he planned to stay until the Second Coming.

Ben got home early. Wendy was so glad to see him, she didn't even realize that she'd dashed to his side and thrown her arms around him until he kissed her soundly and proclaimed, "I like coming home to this!"

When he spied Harry, he stiffened. He tucked Wendy tight to his side. "Thanks for coming to check in on them. I appreciate it."

Harry looked at the two of them. Ben cradled Wendy more closely. She molded to him as if they were made to fit one another. Harry's mouth drooped, and he mumbled, "No problem." He grabbed his bags and plodded out the door.

Wendy slumped. "Whew!"

Ben turned and braced her to himself. He searched her face intently. "Are you all right?"

"She is now," Lael said dryly. "Good thing you got home. Harry hoped you wouldn't, and I was about to take Wendy home with me to keep her out of his reach. The storm is moving in faster than we thought."

"Thanks." Ben's tone of voice underscored his relief and gratitude. "Jack told me the same thing about the blizzard. He took mercy on me and Trent. Since we both have kids at home, he figured neither of us had better get stuck there. He went in early. You should see the supplies he hauled in! He could feed a football team for the season with all of the junk he took."

"We went to town and stocked up on a few things." Lael donned her coat. "I'll get home now, while I can."

"Want me to drive?"

"No, it's still safe. Thanks anyway."

"Call the minute you get in. If you don't contact me in ten minutes, I'll come after you."

Wendy somberly listened to everything. She watched through the window as Lael's Jeep pulled out. Her nerves stretched tighter and tighter until they got the message that Lael made it home safely. "This had better be over soon," Wendy fretted.

Ben's mouth thinned. He said nothing.

Although it had been snowing heavily, nothing fully prepared Wendy for the onslaught of the blizzard. Wind howled and shrieked, and when she peeked out of the window, all she could see was a solid wall of white.

Slipping up from behind, Ben wrapped his arms around her and rested his cheek on her hair. His heat enveloped her, and she stopped shivering in just a few seconds.

"Before I came here, I was stationed on an oil tanker." He

gave her a tiny squeeze. "Storms on the ocean have to be the scariest things going. The ship pitches and yaws until you're hideously sick. If you have to leave your bunk, you get soaking wet. There isn't enough heat around to warm back up even when you change into dry clothes. The water and the sky and the rain are all a churning, angry gray."

"Sounds as if you're not planning to take a cruise sometime soon."

"Not on your life!" He turned her around and cuddled her close. "We're warm here. Safe and warm. The cabin is solid. If you listen carefully, the wind is almost musical. The white is miraculous—so pure, so pristine. Alaska has a wild beauty to it, Wendy. You have to respect it, but you can love it too."

"The old cliché, 'It's a nice place to visit, but I wouldn't want to live there,' comes to mind. Give me sunny, bustling L.A."

He chuckled and hugged her more tightly against himself. "It's nice to know that a mind can be changed."

She leaned away. "I'm not changing my mind, Ben. Alaska might boast great scenery, but I like California's weather far better. I have friends and a great job down there."

"So that welcome home was a show to put Harry off, not 'just because'?"

Wendy looked at the floor and confessed, "I guess I used you. I'm sorry. I really was glad to see you, though. Why don't I bake a cobbler to make it up to you?"

He slid his hand up her nape and cupped the back of her head. He tilted her face to his, canted his head at a comfortable angle, and whispered, "Forget the cobbler. I'll settle for the real thing."

She ducked away and winked. "My cobbler is the real thing!"

He turned away and grumbled, "Shoulda never taught you to polka. You're too good at dancing away."

❧

They tried to make the best of being marooned in the cabin. Ben crowed as loudly as Troy did when the boy moved a few feet forward in his first halting crawl. He enticed him on with squeak toys and played with him incessantly. He was just as likely to tickle Wendy as he was Troy and often tried to spoon a few bites of Troy's baby food into her as he made outrageously rude comments about the look, smell, or texture of the jar's contents.

While the baby napped, they played board games and tried to solve crossword puzzles together. They finished the forget-me-not jigsaw puzzle and put together two others. Their enforced proximity started to wear on her resolve and his control. Slipping past him to toss clothes into the dryer, Wendy found herself drawn into an embrace.

"I want to hold you all of the time," he confessed into her hair. "I even lean toward you so I can smell that sweet scent you wear."

"I'll stop wearing it."

"Don't you dare. It's wonderfully feminine."

She felt her cheeks burn.

Reaching around her, Ben slammed the dryer door shut, then cupped his hands around her waist. He lifted her to sit on the dryer and chuckled. "Gotcha just where I want you." He threaded his fingers through her hair and rubbed noses with her. "I'm dying for a kiss."

"You'd feel that way about any woman after being stranded this long."

"Don't try to explain it away. I know how I feel when we're close."

Easing back from him self-consciously, she muttered, "News flash: You don't always feel that way around me. You've been mad enough to spit nails on occasion and may yet toss me out on my ear in the snow."

Exerting pressure along her spine to draw her close again, Ben growled, "Okay, I'm feeling generous. I'll make a deal. I'll be nice to you all of the time if you're nice to me all of the time." One hand slid up and down her arm, eliciting a firestorm of reactions.

"So good of you to give me some say in the matter," she whispered unevenly, resting her hands on his shoulders.

"That's me all right: a general, all-around good guy." His eyes sparkled as his head dipped closer.

Wendy couldn't resist the attraction any longer. She tilted her face up to his and closed her eyes as their lips met. Being close to him made her feel like her heart had come home. The warmth and caring between them made the contact thrilling, and she felt lost in the moment of being cherished.

Ben shifted, and his leg bumped the dryer. The sound and jarring motion startled Wendy. She jerked away and lifted a shaking hand to her lips. "Why did I do that? I must be crazy—"

"Wendy, you've got to ease up. You're your own worst enemy. What happened between us has been brewing since the moment we met."

"I don't want this!"

"I think you do. It just scares you." He gently stroked back her curls.

"That was. . .it was. . ."

"Beautiful. Rich. Don't regret something so sweet and simple, Wendy. I don't. I can't."

"That's easy for you to say," she wailed.

"Want to make a bet?" When she buried her face in his neck, he fingered her curls and mused, "What now?"

"We have to forget this ever happened," she replied in a muffled tone. "I'll leave just as soon as the plane gets through, and then I can resume a normal life. In the meantime, we'll keep as far apart as possible."

"Why, Sweetie? I think we have something special starting here."

"I think we have something dangerous here. I'm not ready for anything more than a casual friendship, and you're not the marrying type. This was a momentary lapse in sanity brought on by cabin fever. There can't be a next time. As far as I'm concerned, this kind of behavior leads to commitment and children."

His face darkened and he forced her to face him. "Are you saying you wouldn't want to have my child?"

"You don't even want a child! You don't even want Troy!"

"Yes, I do!" he roared back.

Dead silence crackled between them.

Marveling, he repeated himself softly, "Yes, I do. I love that little guy."

ten

Ben and Wendy avidly listened to the weather report the next morning. It wasn't promising in the least. Radar and Doppler studies showed that they had at least five more days of storm. "They just mean snow, right?"

"No, Wendy. It's a full-on blizzard. No one will be going anywhere."

She gave him a horrified look. "How long do these last?"

"I've seen short ones that lasted a day or two and long ones that lasted two weeks."

"Two weeks!"

"We weren't snowed in solid, though. There was a single day-long break before the next one hit. Howie couldn't land, so he did an air drop."

"Two weeks," Wendy moaned, propping herself up against the wall and letting her head thud backward.

"Don't fret. I'll find nice ways to keep busy and warm."

"That's all the more reason for me to worry!"

He comforted her with an embrace. At first, she stayed rigid and fought the attraction, but he was persistent and his hold felt so good that she melted against him and twined her arms around his neck.

He'd put on a CD of oldies, and a man started singing, "Having my baby, what a wonderful way of—"

All of the sudden, Wendy let out a strangled whimper and squirmed desperately. Ben tried to continue to hold her, but she pushed at him. "Sweetie?"

"Let me go," she nearly sobbed.

He obeyed at once. Leaning helplessly into the wall, he watched her bolt across the living room and dash into the bedroom. His head bumped back into the wall.

The night Troy got colic, Ben had gone to the bookshelf and gotten out the impressively large volume on family health. He'd read to discover how to calm an infant. He'd also run across a section on infertility and scanned it.

He gave Wendy a short while, then tapped on the closed bedroom door.

"Go away."

Ignoring her sentiment, he tapped again.

"Why don't you go away?"

Something in her tone got to him. Ben opened the door and sauntered in. He sat on the edge of the bed and played with the sleeve of her shirt. "I understand."

"We're not talking about it."

"Hmm."

"I'm not interested." The pillow rustled as she turned her face away.

"Oh, yes, you are. You're very interested. That makes two of us."

She let out a gasp.

"Did you think I'd be upset to think if things work out between us that we might not be able to have children? Troy is a terrific kid. He'll be enough if you can't have any."

"Stop it!"

"Sweetheart, I know I care about you, and worrying about the future is foolishness. God holds each of our days in His hands."

Wendy sat up and cradled his face between her palms. "You're a special guy, Ben Hawthorne. We talked about praying for wisdom and patience. I think you have plenty of the former."

He chuckled. "Thanks. . .but I'm not sure whether it's Troy or you who's going to teach me more patience!"

She went pink, laughed weakly, and scooted away. "I heard your stomach growl. The only thing you need to be patient about right now is food. I need to get into the kitchen."

He watched as she bashfully headed for the door. She was

trying to run away from him again, and he'd let her. . .for now. Regardless of whether she could bear a child, he wanted her for his wife. A man didn't marry a woman so she could be his brood mare; he wed her to be his love and companion for life. At that moment, he decided coaxing her to see things from his perspective would be a pure joy. "Wendy—"

Troy let out an impatient squawk.

She turned around. "If you'll feed the kid, I'll make something good for sinner—I mean dinner." She blushed profusely.

Letting out a rueful laugh, he asserted, "That was an interesting slip of the tongue."

"Maybe so. Ben, we have to cool things down. I'm not ready for this. You get close, and I lose all sense of reason. I'm not promiscuous."

"Neither of us is." He gave her a lopsided grin.

"What is so amusing?"

"Nothing. Everything. I'm stranded in a cabin in the middle of a blizzard with the most alluring woman I've ever met. The sparks we put off could melt the polar ice cap, and it's not just physical chemistry—it's much deeper than that. Adhering to my Christian morals was never harder. Either I laugh, or I'm going to cry louder and longer than Troy does."

"Then please start laughing." She gave him a tipsy smile. "How about chicken for dinner?"

"Okay."

"Grilled, fried, cacciatore, broiled, Kiev, or with dumplings?"

"Surprise me."

Wendy dissolved into giggles. "I didn't think you liked surprises—the only other surprise I ever sprang on you was Troy, and you got grumpy!"

He smiled. "Give it a try. I'll probably react better this time. I seem to be changing dramatically."

"From footloose bachelor to responsible uncle is a big step."

"From footloose bachelor to serious commitment is a whole lot more enjoyable." He closed the distance between them and squeezed her.

"This is all way too fast for me."

"If you're dizzy, I'm happy to stand here and hold tight."

"The kid will starve."

"All right, I'll feed him while you cook."

As the chicken defrosted in the microwave, Wendy looked in the cupboard and pulled out food for the baby. "Troy," she gushed, "don't you want turkey and vegetables tonight?"

He flapped his hands and cooed.

Ben watched her and crooked a grin at the enthusiastic way she worked with the boy. "If he gets that wound up about chow, what's he going to do when you tell him he gets to wear the squeaky train bib?"

"You tell him."

"I don't think he'll get half as charged up for me. The males of this household seem to prefer you over anything else."

"Oh, give him the bib!" She tried to hide the secret thrill that his words gave her.

"Buster, the lady says you get the train bib." Ben snorted. "See? No reaction. He's sitting there, drooling at me."

"Give it some oomph. Say it the way you think I would."

Ben gave a notably good rendition, and Troy perked up and babbled loudly. He even banged his hands on the tray of the highchair. "Wow! I guess it's all in the delivery."

"He's crazy about you. My brother never got a single squeal out of him, and he doesn't babble half as much to Lael."

"You're not just saying that, are you?"

"No." She gave him a warm smile and started to cook.

Fifteen minutes later, Ben proclaimed, "I got three quarters of this jar into him, and we're only wearing a quarter."

"Congratulations. The two of you make a great team."

After a leisurely supper, they washed the dishes and bathed the baby. "I'm getting pretty good at this," Ben boasted.

"Yes, you are." Wendy turned away. All of the sudden, her joy went flat. Troy didn't need her any longer. Neither did Ben. She'd done what she'd set out to do—bring the baby to his uncle and ensure that they'd manage well. She'd always taken pride in finishing jobs and doing her best, but this time, it broke her heart.

"Ben, do you mind if I call Bruce?"

"Go ahead."

Wendy wished there was a phone elsewhere, but Ben only had one in the kitchen. She dialed and mentally calculated her brother should be home from the office by now.

"Hey, Sis, when are you getting home?"

"As soon as the blizzard lets up."

"It better be soon. Listen, I have bad news: Your boss isn't happy at all about you being gone this long."

"I can't help it. What did he say?" She drew in a quick breath at the memory of the penthouse-level restaurant where she worked. Expensive and exclusive, it catered to clientele who appreciated fine dining and didn't mind picking up a hefty tab. If she lost her position there, she'd never move out on her own.

Bruce went on, "He sounded frazzled. Reminded me he only gave you a couple days off to drop off Troy."

"I know he only gave me three days off, but stuff has come up. I can't control the weather."

"Yeah, well, I was just passing on the message. Since the phone is working, call him tomorrow. Oh—I'm supposed to tell you Vicky's having a going-away party for Rena and Chris. I got the idea she'd like you to help out with the food. She said Chris got transferred to New York. And Deb is counting on you to make baby-shower cakes for Kelly and someone else. I guess you're going to be busy, huh?"

"It sounds like it." Bruce asked about Troy and Ben, then needed to get ready for a date. Wendy hung up and wiped down the already-clean kitchen counter. Thoughts whirled through her mind, but she couldn't put them in order.

Everyone else is paired up like the animals on Noah's Ark. Two by two. I'm making wedding and baby-shower cakes for everybody I know. Bruce and Lacey will probably get engaged soon. I'll go home to a great job, but I'll be sitting home alone at night when everyone else has someone. What I really want—who I really want—is up here.

She shivered—but it wasn't just because of the cold.

Wendy slipped to her room and reappeared, wearing a sweatshirt over her turtleneck. Ben sat forward and his brows knit. She wouldn't look at him, because if she did, she'd start crying. Since Troy had fallen asleep, she carefully covered him up in the playpen.

Ben patted the couch next to him. "Come on over."

"I'm tired."

"We can watch an old movie."

"No, thank you." Without another word, she went to the kitchen, swallowed some aspirin, and turned back around. Once she got to the bedroom, she quietly shut the door, changed, and crept into the bed.

After that, she stayed secluded in her room. When she slid out at noon to use the bathroom, Ben invited, "I made us ham sandwiches. Want to eat at the table, or should we have a picnic in front of the fireplace again?"

"I'm not hungry."

"Then keep me company."

"Not now." She withdrew to her room. Too many feelings buffeted her for her to sort them out. How could she leave Troy and Ben? Returning to work at Papier Luné should make her ecstatic, but she really didn't care. What good would it be, to cook for strangers and go home to a lonely, empty apartment?

Ben was right about Caribou Crossing—the population was small; then again, how many people did she really socialize with back home? Folks at church appreciated all of her help in the kitchen for showers and events, and she had a small circle of good friends, but in the past year, most of the gals had gotten married or had a baby and weren't available to do things. By contrast, folks here in Alaska formed a true, old-fashioned community where everyone mattered and counted on one another. They'd welcomed her with open arms, and everyone had made it clear they hoped she'd stay.

If only Ben would tell her he wanted her to stay. It had been a whole year since Larry broke their engagement, and for the first time, she'd found peace and true happiness here. It wasn't the place—it was the company. . .Ben's company.

Something in the corner caught her eye—a puzzle box. Forget-me-not. Wendy bit back a cry.

Her prayers were disjointed. Finally, she whispered, "Lord, I don't know what to do. Show me the way."

In the wee hours of the morning, she finally curled up on her bed and fell asleep.

"You didn't sleep much last night, did you?" a silky voice inquired as she began to stir sometime later.

"Unh-unh." She opened her eyes blearily and blinked. Something wasn't quite right, but it took a few minutes before she recognized the fact that Ben was leaning over her.

He brushed her hair aside and kissed her temple. "I like the way you smile when you sleep."

"What are you doing here?"

"Checking on you. I knocked three times, but you didn't answer, and I wanted to be sure you weren't sick or something. It's not like you to sleep in."

"I'm fine."

"Sweetie, I don't know what to do. Troy desperately needs you to care for him, and I love him. It's my responsibility to make sure he's taken care of, and as his guardian, I'm more than relieved that you're able to do it."

"Please—"

His fingers gently pressed her mouth, holding back the words. "Sweetie, you run away when you're troubled. That's not going to work for us. We have to talk things out. Let me finish, and then I'll give you your say."

"Give me a minute. I'll meet you in the living room."

❧

Ben scarcely waited for her to sit in one of the blue chairs.

"I'm torn. I didn't mean to eavesdrop, but I know your boss is giving you grief. I want you to be happy, and I know you love city life and want to do fancy gourmet stuff.

"Still, what you and Troy share is unbelievably sweet. Severing that bond is a terrible thing to do. It's breaking your heart to think of leaving him here. You've spent the last twenty-four hours hiding away from us, trying to separate and guard your heart. I love it up here, but if it would ease your heart, I'll look for a job down in L.A."

"Ben!"

"I'm serious."

"I know you feel like you still need help taking care of Troy—"

He held up his hand. "Hold on a minute here. I'm not looking for a baby-sitter. Lael can fill that job just fine. I'm talking about us—you and me. Troy kind of figures into the equation simply because he brought us together."

He couldn't be quite sure, but he thought he heard her mumble, "Forget-me-not."

"I know how scared you are, Wendy, and I don't blame you. Your engagement was a disaster, but I'll never see you as anything other than a complete woman. How could I do otherwise, when I love you? I want to lock you in here with us, but if you don't want to live in Alaska, I'll move. I know we'd be happy, but I can't control you, and I can't demand anything. All I can say is that we love you and need you."

"You do?"

"Yes, Wendy." His hands gently cupped her waist. He smiled. "I never believed in love at first sight or whirlwind romances, but that's exactly what's happened to me."

"But you don't know. . ."

"I think I do," he said softly.

She shook her head miserably. Her eyes brimmed with tears. "I might not be able to give you a child."

Ben's heart flipped. *Lord, how could anyone have hurt or betrayed her so deeply? Give me the words to reassure her, to tell her what's in my heart.*

He kissed her hair. "Honey, we've been over this. You already gave me Troy. You're more woman than I've ever known. Having a baby isn't what makes you a woman. It's your tender heart and loving ways. I never dreamed I'd find anyone like you." He smiled. "It took a real woman to tame a rough, old Alaskan bachelor.

"You already told me the doctor said your chances of having a baby are slim," he continued. "We might conceive; we might not. If we do, we'll have a house full of kids. If we don't, I'll love you and Troy every bit as much and never have a single regret."

He kissed her fingertips. When she shivered, he whispered, "I can't promise everything will be perfect between us, Wendy. I know I won't ever betray you or leave you, and with Christ as the cornerstone of our family, we'll be building our relationship on solid ground. I know I'll love Troy too."

Too? He loved Troy too. . .how was she supposed to interpret that? That he was reminding her of what he'd said awhile back when he declared he shared the love she had for the baby. . .or did he mean he loved her as well as the baby? She felt a sense of elation, then fright. "You're going too fast."

"Too fast? Okay. So do you want me to do a long-distance courtship on the computer and telephone? Do you want me to build a cabin next door for you? What are you looking for?"

"I don't know. I thought everything I wanted was back home, but last night I realized that isn't true." She gave him a wobbly smile. "Other than the sunshine."

"Soon we'll have sun at midnight. You'll get plenty." His smile could light a stadium. "We'll add on this spring. It means we won't have enough time to go on a long honeymoon, though."

"Honeymoon?"

"Okay, a family trip," he groused. "I guess I can't expect to leave Troy behind. On our first anniversary, I expect a private getaway, though."

"Ben, you want to get married?"

"Of course I do. What do you think this whole conversation has been about?"

"You told me you were a confirmed bachelor, that you didn't want a family."

"And later, I told you that who I was and what I wanted were changing. I can't imagine a day without both of you in my life, and I don't want to think of a night without cuddling you."

"As much as I wanted Troy for myself, I realized he needed to be with you. God wouldn't give me peace about taking him away."

Ben chortled. "Yeah, but I knew Troy and you shouldn't ever be parted. God kept stopping you from leaving. Once I hauled you out of the plane when Chuck broke his leg, I sensed the Lord might well be working something special in our lives."

"So we get each other, and we both keep Troy."

Ben nodded. "His plans are always so much better than we can dream up. We just have to put our trust in Him." Letting out a chuckle, he cupped her cheek. "Before you consent to anything, you have to know something, just in case a miracle happens. Twins run in my family."

Wendy tipped her head back and giggled.

eleven

They snuggled on the couch after supper, and Troy began to fuss. Wendy reached to take him. "Fork him over. It's my turn to calm him down."

"Are you sure?"

She nodded. "All night and through the morning, I agonized over this. I felt so guilty. You see, I was afraid that I was cheating you and him if I stayed. You've made me understand that if we love one another, things will fall into place. If I left, the two of you might kill one another off. . .you'd die of sleep deprivation, or he'd get knocked off because of you doing something totally crazy."

"Nope. We'd likely die of plain old boring starvation."

Propping a hand on her hip, she huffed, "I should have known it. Howie Kalman brought me just so I'd be your cook!"

He chuckled. "So you're okay with everything now?"

"I think so."

"We'll call Doc Michaelson tomorrow to make appointments for both of you. I'll have to start making phone calls here in a few minutes. You need to call your boss and quit. Your brother'll have to pack up all of your things and send them right away."

"Aren't you moving pretty fast?"

"Nope." He gave her a big grin. "I'm going to tell Howie to bring in the pastor. What size do you wear?"

"Why?"

"He'll bring in a wedding dress for you—unless you'd rather fly to Fairbanks for the wedding and have it in a real church."

"Why? I don't know a soul in Fairbanks. If we do it here, you can have a couple of your friends be our witnesses. What do we do for a license?"

"Chuck went through all of this two years ago. Wila Pern is the county registrar, and her husband is the mayor and a lay pastor. Since we don't have a clinic, they wave the blood tests and issue a license to anyone who's interested. It's pretty rinky-dink, but if the state audits us, we're legit."

"I met Wila at Janet's the day the blizzard hit."

"I know." Ben chuckled. "But she'd already heard all about you. The day after Susan and Betty visited you, Wila came to the pump station and gave me a jewelry catalog. I got orders from her to choose a wedding ring for you, so I don't think she'll give us any guff about wanting a marriage license."

"You're kidding me!"

"Am I?" He stood and went to the desk. He rifled through a stack of papers and brought back two catalogs. Tossing one down on the floor, he decided, "We'll look at that one tomorrow. Now as for rings. . ."

"I don't believe this," Wendy chortled.

"Get used to it, Sweetie. We shop from catalogs a lot." He flipped to the back of the jewelry book and inquired, "What do you like—platinum, white gold, or yellow gold?"

"Yellow."

"What shape diamond?" He held the pages open for her and stabbed at a few. "Round? Square? Football?"

"Football!" She tilted back her head and laughed until she cried. As she settled down, she wiped her eyes and breathlessly begged, "Forgive me, Ben. It's just that those are called marquis cut."

"Marquis," he groused. "Looks like a football to me. What is this one? Teardrop?"

"Pear."

"Now I know why jewelers wear those funny glasses with the magnifying glass side car. They're practically blind! Pear!"

He got started and wouldn't let loose of the topic. He snorted when she described diamonds as being channel set or pavé, and when she uttered "baguette," he objected, "You had a fit over "football," and they name those after a silly loaf of bread!"

Resting her head on his shoulder, she giggled helplessly.

He kissed her. "See? Catalog shopping can be kind of fun."

❧

The next day, they sat down to make a shopping list for Ben to e-mail in. Ben had a production of setting pens, a few pads of paper, and the pot of coffee on the table before they set to work.

"Ben, just how long do you think it's going to take to make a shopping list?"

"A long time, Sweetie. We have to think carefully. After a blizzard, everyone orders something they discovered they'd forgotten. Space on the plane will be tight, so we have to prioritize."

"Just what does that entail?"

"I'm afraid it means we'll be cutting back to bare bones this time. Our other pilot, Abe Hunters, used to simply do air drops to help take up the slack after a bad spell of weather, but he's out of the picture. We have to make a list of absolutes and carefully estimate how much space they'll take. We have to remember that everyone else in Caribou Crossing needs supplies, and Howie's plane isn't all that big."

Chewing on her lip, she nodded. She grabbed a pen and began a list. "Powdered formula. Two cases."

"That's too much, Wendy. One case is absolute. We'll request three more on standby, and Howie will try to get them in during the next week." He lifted the top sheet of paper from her pad and ripped the next one out. Giving her the original list, he explained, "I'll keep a second list going. It'll have all of the other supplies we want. Most will get here in the next week. We all give Howie these scraps of paper—he calls 'em 'Gimmie quicks'—and he tries to honor whatever he can when he has the space."

"How does he determine who to let have the space?"

"Folks here are pretty laid back, Wendy. Since it's Howie's plane, he can decide whatever he wants. He's surprisingly diplomatic. If someone gets something this time, chances are good that he brings in something for someone else the next.

He had a good sense of urgency, though. We did get the crib and highchair right away."

"You do realize that Bruce will be sending all of my gear up here. I'll ask him to send a changing table too."

"It would be nice to have the coffee table back."

"Not for long. Troy will be walking in about three months. He'll knock everything off of it. Speaking of coffee, we're almost out. Is that a first list or a second?"

"If you ask me, the only necessities that rate higher are toilet paper, diapers, formula, and Cookie."

She scribbled those down and inquired, "What kind of cookies?"

"Not cookies, Wendy, Cookie. You. I want you, and I'll savor you from now to eternity." He twisted one of her curls around his finger and tugged her closer. She offered no resistance at all, and they wasted more than a few minutes with an ardent kiss.

By lunchtime, they finished drafting their list. Wendy sat next to Ben as he typed everything in on a computerized order form. Once they'd completed everything, she commented, "I think I'll go up to the attic and grab a few things. I've been toying with an idea for supper."

"Fine by me." He walked her to the hatch and pulled it down. While she was in the attic, Ben slinked to the phone and quietly sent in one last order.

That evening, they sat on the couch and looked through the second catalog Ben had gotten out. It was from the log cabin company, and they tried to decide which style to purchase.

"If we build upward, we won't have to worry about expanding the foundation," Ben pointed out, looking at the possible packages that would add a second story.

"I'm not crazy about the idea of stairs with Troy around," Wendy protested as she propped Troy up on her lap. "I'd much rather build out than up any day."

Ben gave her a wry smile. "You're only saying that because you don't want the attic torn off and the mess everywhere while we go up."

"I hadn't given that a single thought, but it certainly bolsters my opinion!"

"Just how many children are we going to have? That will affect our decision as to how many more square feet we need."

Thoroughly entertained, Wendy leaned into him and started to laugh.

"What's so funny?"

"You are! The first time you saw this kid, you turned a sickly shade of puce and bellowed that you didn't like children; yet now you're wondering about how many more we can wedge under the roof, and I'm worried that I can't give them to you!"

"Rub it in, why don't you?" he groused without a trace of embarrassment or anger.

"If anything, I'd think your knees ought to be rubbed. The way you crawled around on the floor with Troy had to bang them up pretty badly."

He grinned at her. "It was worth it. We had a great time." He tickled Troy's tummy and said, "You tell her, Buster. Tell her love is worth the bumps and bruises and being considerate is what smooths out the rough parts."

"I thought you said you didn't know anything about being married."

"No, I didn't." He took Troy from her. "What I said was, I didn't want to get married because I'd seen my father's relationships all fail. I've been doing a lot of thinking about it since you got here. The pivotal points were that God wasn't ever part of his marriages, and Dad never respected the women he was with. They weren't any better because they were along for whatever financial benefits he could provide."

"That sounds pretty cold."

"Truth isn't always pretty. If he and his wife or girlfriend weren't kissing, they were fighting."

"We've done a fair amount of fighting," she pointed out quietly.

He surprised her by chuckling. She fully expected him to be unsettled by that observation. "True. We have."

"Where does that leave us?"

"Wendy, we've gotten hit with some of life's biggest blows and still managed to settle each issue as it's come up. Some of the solutions were immediate, and others took time. The fact that we fell in love in the middle of that is astonishing."

"Miraculous."

He nodded. "You've allowed me to change, and I've given you a chance to let go of some of the hurt you've carried around. We've both had to adjust to opening our hearts to each other and Troy."

"I don't think we're anywhere near done adjusting."

"Probably not. Caring for a kid and adding on will certainly bring up the most important issues right away. So far, we've done okay."

She giggled. "How could we have fallen in love?"

His arms tightened around her. "If we've learned to love one another in the midst of everything so far, with God's help, I figure we can weather just about anything."

"I think maybe I can weather anything except this weather. I'm going stir crazy."

"I think it's cozy, Sweetie. Maybe the house is cramped, but we'll add on. Lael is happy to come help, and we can count on her to continue with that. She was delighted to be able to baby-sit Troy. Between Troy and me, we'll keep you busy. You won't have a chance to be bored."

Twisting her head around, she teased, "What? You don't want me to cook?"

He spread his hands wide. "What do you want me to say? God blessed me with a woman of many talents."

❧

Three days later, the blizzard let up. Chuck Pearson returned wearing a cast. A strange looking affair that strongly resembled a garbage bag was wrapped over it to protect it from the snow.

"Ben, he can't go to work like that," Wendy whispered to him. "I hadn't given a thought to the fact that the snow would make it too precarious for him to hobble on crutches. Janet is home on bed rest. He needs to stay there with her."

"Sweetie, you have to understand that if he doesn't report for work, I have to stay. We won't be able to go on that family honeymoon."

Walking her fingers up the buttons of his shirt, she looked up at him through her lashes. "I think we can improvise. What about you?"

Cupping his hands around her waist, he hoarsely asked, "How long does it take to shake the wrinkles out of a wedding gown?"

Everyone milled around the landing strip and claimed the supplies that were flown in. They loaded them into cars and took them home. At noon, they all returned to the town meeting hall. There was no room on the plane for another passenger, so Bruce couldn't come up and the minister wasn't there to perform the wedding ceremony. Mr. Pern officiated.

Ben sent away for flowers when he made his secret radio call, so even with a casted leg, Chuck had patiently carried the large box on his lap. Lael and Wila had spent the morning making arrangements with them and putting up white streamers. Ben even thought to order a sheaf of white roses with forget-me-nots for Wendy to carry. She was so deeply touched when she saw them, she started to cry.

"None of that," Wila teased gently. "Your makeup will run!"

To Wendy's relief, both the gown and the rings fit. Harry insisted on walking her down the aisle, and Lael stood in as matron of honor. Wendy noticed none of the details—she was too captivated by the love in Ben's eyes and voice to care.

The ceremony ended with a sweet kiss, and the ladies of Caribou Crossing gave them a brief luncheon reception. Although everyone would have enjoyed staying and celebrating longer, another storm loomed on the horizon and prudence won over partying.

Once the bride and groom got home, Ben ordered, "You stay put." He got out of the car they'd borrowed and took Troy inside. He came back out and swept Wendy into his arms. He carried her to the threshold and stopped.

"God's given me so much, Wendy. You came up here with an unexpected delivery, but in truth, you were the hidden gift in His plan. I love you, Sweetheart. Welcome home."

epilogue

Wendy dropped a few bags from her shopping trip in Seattle and went outside. "I'm home!"

Ben stuck his head around the side of the wooden fort, but a chorus of high-pitched war whoops drowned out his response.

Wendy leaned over the porch railing and laughed. "Do my eyes deceive me, or is my husband running a day care?"

Ben snagged a little black-haired boy off a climbing rope and set him back down. "Janet is sick, and Chuck had to work. I volunteered to watch their boys."

Five years ago, Wendy wouldn't have believed this to be possible, but Ben had turned into a regular Pied Piper. When Janet had her second son, Wendy had struggled again with hungering for a baby, but Ben never wavered in his love and acceptance for her. God had given them each other and Troy—and that was more than enough for him to feel blessed. Though they hadn't used any precautions, Wendy still hadn't conceived when Janet gave birth to a third boy. Instead of dwelling on what they didn't have, Wendy and Ben became "aunt and uncle" to Chuck and Janet's three sons; so at the moment, they had four noisy, grubby, adorable little kids in their backyard.

"Ben, what on earth are you wearing?"

Ben smiled over at her and gave a nail one more whack. "My tool belt."

"Nifty assortment of tools you have there, Mr. Hawthorne." She studied the loops and pouch with undisguised interest. "Hmm. Hammer, nails, tape measure, diaper, bottle. . ."

"Everything to get the job done." He stood and pushed a toddler in the bucket swing he'd hung from a rafter. "I've got everything under control."

Wendy came down the steps of a huge porch and into the yard. With their neighbors' help, they'd added on another room and a bathroom that first summer. The addition was finished just in time for a visit from Wendy's brother. Bruce had thrown a magnificent house-warming party for them, complete with food he'd brought up on dry ice that he'd ordered from the restaurant where Wendy had once worked. Since then, Bruce had come for a visit each summer, and he'd helped add on the porch.

Troy dashed up and gave her a hug, then ran off with the other boys. Wendy glanced back at the house, then mused, "You think you have everything under control? I don't know about that."

Ben raised his brows, then pursed his lips and looked at the cabin. "Did I miss something?"

She watched as his big hands gently gave the bucket swing another nudge.

"Well?" Ben prodded.

"I was thinking. . .I'd like to add on a little more."

"Really?" He crammed the hammer into his tool belt. "Sweetheart, you'll need to wait 'til next summer. We won't have time."

"Waiting 'til next summer is out of the question. I have a special addition in mind." She pulled a small sales brochure from her pocket and handed it to him. She'd taken the Eagleson's log cabin ad and pasted Troy's picture over the "Little Guy" model.

Ben smiled. He opened it, then looked at the next page and let out a joyous whoop. Over the picture of the "Baby" model, Wendy had pasted a pink-and-blue striped piece of paper. "By God's infinite grace: Baby Hawthorne, expected delivery on Valentine's Day."

A Letter To Our Readers

Dear Reader:

In order that we might better contribute to your reading enjoyment, we would appreciate your taking a few minutes to respond to the following questions. We welcome your comments and read each form and letter we receive. When completed, please return to the following:

Rebecca Germany, Fiction Editor
Heartsong Presents
PO Box 719
Uhrichsville, Ohio 44683

1. Did you enjoy reading *Hand Quilted with Love* by Joyce Livingston?

    ❏ Very much! I would like to see more books by this author!

    ❏ Moderately. I would have enjoyed it more if

    _____

    _____

2. Are you a member of **Heartsong Presents**? Yes ❏ No ❏
    If no, where did you purchase this book?_____

    _____

3. How would you rate, on a scale from 1 (poor) to 5 (superior), the cover design?_____

4. On a scale from 1 (poor) to 10 (superior), please rate the following elements.

    _____ Heroine   _____ Plot

    _____ Hero   _____ Inspirational theme

    _____ Setting   _____ Secondary characters

5. These characters were special because_____

_____

_____

6. How has this book inspired your life?_____

_____

_____

7. What settings would you like to see covered in future
   Heartsong Presents books?_____

_____

_____

8. What are some inspirational themes you would like to see
   treated in future books?_____

_____

_____

9. Would you be interested in reading other **Heartsong
   Presents** titles?   Yes ❑   No ❑

10. Please check your age range:
    ❑ Under 18   ❑ 18-24   ❑ 25-34
    ❑ 35-45   ❑ 46-55   ❑ Over 55

Name _____

Occupation _____

Address _____

City _____ State _____ Zip _____

Email _____

········Presents·······

Great Inspirational Romance at a Great Price!

Heartsong Presents books are inspirational romances in contemporary and historical settings, designed to give you an enjoyable, spirit-lifting reading experience. You can choose wonderfully written titles from some of today's best authors like Hannah Alexander, Irene B. Brand, Yvonne Lehman, Tracie Peterson, and many others.

When ordering quantities less than twelve, above titles are $2.95 each.
Not all titles may be available at time of order.

Heartsong Presents
Love Stories
Are Rated G!

That's for godly, gratifying, and of course, great! If you love a thrilling love story but don't appreciate the sordidness of some popular paperback romances, **Heartsong Presents** is for you. In fact, **Heartsong Presents** is the *only inspirational romance book club* featuring love stories where Christian faith is the primary ingredient in a marriage relationship.

Sign up today to receive your first set of four never-before-published Christian romances. Send no money now; you will receive a bill with the first shipment. You may cancel at any time without obligation, and if you aren't completely satisfied with any selection, you may return the books for an immediate refund!

Imagine. . .four new romances every four weeks—two historical, two contemporary—with men and women like you who long to meet the one God has chosen as the love of their lives. . .all for the low price of $9.97 postpaid.

To join, simply complete the coupon below and mail to the address provided. **Heartsong Presents** romances are rated G for another reason: They'll arrive *Godspeed!*

www.heartsongpresents.com